Now a
Harlequin
romance
by Anne Mather
comes to life
on the movie screen

starring
KEIR DULLEA · SUSAN PENHALIGON

Leopard in the Snow

Guest Stars
KENNETH MORE · BILLIE WHITELAW

featuring GORDON THOMSON as MICHAEL
and JEREMY KEMP as BOLT

Produced by JOHN QUESTED and CHRIS HARROP
Screenplay by ANNE MATHER and JILL HYEM
Directed by GERRY O'HARA
An Anglo-Canadian Co-Production

OTHER
Harlequin Romances
by FLORA KIDD

Many of these titles are available at your local bookseller,
or through the Harlequin Reader Service.

For a free catalogue listing all available Harlequin Romances,
send your name and address to:

HARLEQUIN READER SERVICE,
M.P.O. Box 707, Niagara Falls, N.Y. 14302
Canadian address: Stratford, Ontario, Canada N5A 6W4

or use order coupon at back of books.

To Play
with Fire

by

FLORA KIDD

Harlequin Books

TORONTO • LONDON • NEW YORK • AMSTERDAM • SYDNEY

Original hardcover edition published in 1977
by Mills & Boon Limited

ISBN 0-373-02146-1

Harlequin edition published March 1978

PRINTED IN U.S.A.

CHAPTER ONE

TORY smelt the island before she ever saw it. Her sensitive nose picked up the fragrance of many flowers and spices wafted towards her on a warm breeze which ruffled the blue sea.

Eagerly she scanned the hazy horizon. Suddenly the haze shifted to become a cloud which lifted and was whisked away as a gauzy handkerchief is whisked away by the hand of a magician, to reveal the blue-grey slopes of a flat-topped mountain towering over the rolling green countryside of the island of Airouna.

The cloud gone, the sun shone more brightly out of a cobalt blue sky. The sea changed colour from slate blue to a deep turquoise, pinpointed with silvery light; a light which increased in power and became a hot bright glare so that Tory was forced to find her sunglasses and put them on.

Through the tinted lenses she was able to make out details of the island. A white lighthouse stood on a point of land, and beyond the point a wide bay opened up rimmed by sparkling white sand overhung by lush tropical vegetation. At the head of the bay was a cluster of white red-roofed buildings backed by a hillside covered by forest. As the ferry boat which had brought her from Antigua swept into the bay, Tory saw other buildings curving round one shore half-hidden by the torn-umbrella shapes of palm trees and the delicate feather-branches of casuarinas.

The ferry's engines slowed down as it approached a big red navigation buoy which moved up and down on the waves with a slow stern majesty. Carefully the ferry rounded the buoy and gathered speed again, passing a black sailing schooner which was taking advantage of the off-shore breeze to run out to sea, its sails shimmering in the sunlight. Tory had a glimpse of its cabin roof bright with yellow paint, of the man at its wheel, his legs braced against the heaving deck, his dark-skinned face split by a wide grin as he raised a hand in greeting to someone on the ferry. Then the schooner had gone, its wide wake making a smooth path of flat water.

The entrance to the harbour of Port Anne lay between two points of land crowded with buildings. Most of them were the original warehouses built by English merchants in the eighteenth century. Painted white, with round-topped doorways, rectangular upper windows edged by brightly painted shutters, and with steeply sloping roofs of red pantiles, their shabby elegance was offset by the crude angular design of modern concrete buildings which clustered behind them.

Since the harbour was crowded with fishing boats and small pleasure craft the ferry had some difficulty in approaching its berth, but after a great deal of shouting by captain and crew, of reversing and advancing of its engines, it bumped against the stone wall of the wide wharf at last.

There was a small group of people standing on the wharf waiting for the ferry and beyond them Tory could see a wide road skirting a square planted with circles of grass edged by borders of bright flowers and shaded by graceful Royal palms.

'Tory, Tory!'

Hearing her name being shouted, she looked down at the group of people again. A man who was wearing conventional khaki shorts, a white shirt and a floppy white sunhat was waving to her. She recognised him at once. He was Dr Magnus Jarrold, director of the Airounian Botanical Gardens, famous botanist and

6

one-time professor of the science at the university at which she had taken her degree, whose summons had brought her to work for him as an assistant botanist on this Caribbean island.

Feeling a surge of excitement because she had arrived at last, Tory waved back, then turned quickly, intent on finding her luggage and going ashore. In her hurry she walked straight into someone who was passing along the deck behind her. It was like colliding with the rock of Gibraltar. Breath hissed out of her as the violence of the collision jarred her from head to foot.

'Oh, I'm sorry,' she gasped as she regained her balance by clutching hold of his brawny bare forearm. 'I'm afraid I wasn't looking where I was going.'

'Obviously you weren't or you wouldn't have walked into me. I'm not exactly wraith-like.'

He certainly wasn't. Although not much taller than herself, he gave the impression of being big and solid. His voice had a hard cutting edge to it as if he were used to giving orders and its accent, though different, was as English as her own.

Withdrawing her hand from the man's sun-bronzed forearm, she looked up into hazel eyes which were deepset between dark lashes under thick dark eyebrows: eyes which flickered and danced with a bright wicked light. Under the right eye was a greenish-looking bruise, and above the right eyebrow a pad of white lint was held in place over some sort of wound by strips of sticking plaster. He looked as if he'd been in a fight.

His hair was dark brown, thick and curly, close-cropped, and grew in long sideburns down his lean cheeks.

Under a gaily-patterned open-necked short-sleeved shirt his wide shoulders were hunched because he was resting on wooden crutches, and Tory felt a twinge of

7

conscience as her glance travelled downwards over long legs clothed in white cotton pants to the sandalled right foot which was being held clear of contact with the deck.

Now she remembered seeing him come aboard at Antigua. He had arrived in a taxi at the wharf from which the ferryboat had left. The captain of the ferryboat had greeted him like an old friend with a laughing ribald remark which had been answered by an equally rude, succinct observation which had made Tory's ears tingle with embarrassment because she was not accustomed to hearing such forthright language.

'I hope I didn't hurt you,' she said now in an effort to ease the twinge of conscience. He was standing directly in front of her, blocking the entrance to the ferryboat's saloon in which she had left her luggage.

'You didn't, I'm glad to say,' he replied coolly, his bright glance roving over her boldly. 'With that corn-silk hair your eyes should be cornflower blue. Are they?'

She stiffened. The nerve of the man, thinking he could make personal comments just because she had walked into him! He was obviously the bold buccaneering type who didn't hesitate to make a pass at a woman, given the slightest opportunity. Well, he was going to learn that his daring tactics were wasted on her! She was immune to openly-admiring glances and frank comments about the colour of her hair.

'No, they're not, they're grey,' she snapped, hoping that he would take a hint from the coldness of her voice and move out of her way.

But he stayed right where he was and seemed more amused than ever.

'Now's that's a pity,' he drawled. 'You see, I've always wanted to know a woman with yellow hair and blue eyes. Apart from the eyes you look as if you'd suit my purpose admirably.'

8

'What purpose?' she demanded, intrigued in spite of her resolve to freeze him.

'I'm looking for a woman with whom to share my bed and board,' he said outrageously. 'A woman like you.'

Only the facts that he was on crutches, had a black eye and a cut above his eyebrow saved him from having his face slapped by Tory's large well-shaped competent hand. Controlling herself with a great effort, she said between her set teeth,

'You're either drunk or crazy. Now will you please move out of the way so that I can go into the saloon to collect my luggage?'

He didn't move, nor did he look ashamed.

'I admit to having had a couple of drinks since I came aboard, but I'm not drunk,' he said clearly, 'and I'm usually considered to be more sane than most people around here. Why you should consider me to be drunk or crazy just because I'm honest I can't understand, but I'm glad to hear you're going ashore here. It means that for once the powers that be are on my side and we were fated to meet.'

The remark jolted her and she flicked a wary glance in his direction. He noticed and his sudden grin was a startling white flash in his wind-burned, dark face.

'Aha, that struck a spark,' he scoffed softly. 'Like many women you're a fatalist.'

'No, I'm not,' she flashed. 'I believe each one of us is in control of our own lives.'

'Will you be staying long on the island?'

'I've come to work here,' she snapped.

'That's a surprise. Anyone meeting you?'

'Yes.'

'Who?'

'It's no business of yours,' she seethed. 'Now will you

9

please move. I'd like to get off this boat before it departs for the next island.'

'Oh, there's plenty of time. No one hurries in the islands—that's something you'll have to learn and accept if you're going to live here. You might as well tell me who's meeting you, because I'm going to find out anyway when I go ashore here too,' he said coolly.

Tory had the strangest feeling of being trapped in that moment of time, as if she would stand there for ever feeling the hot sun scorching her skin, hearing the soft lilting cadence of West Indian speech and song as the crewmen unloaded supplies from the boat to the wharf, knowing that Magnus was waiting for her yet unable to join him because she was being held prisoner by a rude, overbearing ruffian.

Dark as he was, with those wickedly glinting eyes, his big shoulders hunched over the crutches, he seemed like one of the ruthless marauding pirates who had once dominated the seas around the islands and who was determined to hold her hostage. She saw him as immovable, rock-like, coming between her and Magnus, preventing her from meeting the man for whom she had left country, family and friends as well as a safe job.

'If you don't let me pass at once I'll scream for help,' she cried out, driven to desperation by a feeling of panic.

Amusement fled from his face. It left his eyes as clear and as hard as an eagle's. Involuntarily she stepped backward from him, and his mouth twisted cynically.

'There's no need for you to back away. I'm not going to touch you, even though you should be given a good hiding for what you've just implied,' he sneered.

'I wasn't ... I didn't intend to imply anything,' she defended. 'I just want to pass, please.'

'And I was just showing a friendly interest in a newcomer to the island,' he retorted. 'Okay, you can pass. I'm sorry I bothered.'

He swung out of her way. Released, Tory scurried past him without a word of excuse. The brief clash of personalities had made her quiver with indignation. He was sorry he had bothered, was he? She felt she would choke with the anger which surged up like sickness as she realised how deftly he had turned the tables on her by making out that she was the offender because she had rejected his offer of friendship.

Now that the ferryboat was at rest and there was no passage of air through its ventilators, the saloon was oppressively hot. Feeling sweat break out on her skin as she hurried, Tory found her cases, picked them up and lugged them out and along the deck to the gangway. By the time she stepped off the gangway on to the sun-baked stones of the quayside her blue-flowered cotton dress was soaked with sweat at the armholes and she was wishing she had taken the time to put on the sunhat which was in her canvas holdall.

But Magnus was there, his hands outstretched in greeting, his light blue eyes smiling at her from under the brim of the floppy hat. All was right with her world again, so she dropped the cases, placed her hands in his and leaned forward to kiss him on the cheek.

'Tory, my dear, how wonderful it is to see you!' he said as he returned her kiss. His voice was just as she remembered it, soft and gentle, with the slightest of guttural accents because he was Danish by birth.

'It's wonderful to be here at last,' she replied sincerely. She glanced round at the colourful scene; brilliant blue water, sparkling white walls, glowing red roofs—under the bright tropical sunshine everything seemed more intense, more vital. 'I can hardly believe I'm here,' she said. 'Oh, Magnus, you've no idea how glad I was when your letter came. I was beginning to think ...'

'That I'd forgotten about you,' he put in gently. 'I know, and I regret the delay, but it wasn't my fault.

Because it was a government appointment there were certain formalities to go through. But now you're here and I'd like you to meet my daughter Carla. I hope you and she are going to be friends. Carla, this is Tory Latham.'

His daughter! Tory hoped she wasn't showing that his announcement had shattered her. She stared at the small dark-haired girl whom he drew forward. Olive-skinned and black-eyed, Carla was wearing a simple sundress made from colour-splashed white cotton which left her back bare to the waist and plunged low at the front to give glimpses of dusky-skinned rounded breasts.

Her smile feeling strained and false, Tory held out a hand in greeting, but Carla did not seem to notice it and after a brief casual nod looked past Tory at someone or something beyond her. At once the slanting, opaque black eyes lit up with pleasure.

'Denzil!' she called out. 'Oh, look, he's on crutches. Daddy, don't go yet, I want to ask Denzil what he's been doing to get hurt.'

'Carla, never mind ...' Magnus broke off and shrugged his narrow shoulders helplessly as his daughter disregarded his protest completely, and danced off in the direction of the gangway down which the dark man was swinging on his crutches.

Magnus turned back to Tory, a slightly wry smile pulling his mouth sideways.

'She's very impulsive, and to tell you the truth I'm worried about her. She's seventeen and has just discovered men.' He sighed heavily and his forehead puckered anxiously; Tory wanted to smooth it. 'The man you see over there on the crutches is one man I wish she had never discovered,' he added in a discouraged way.

'Who is he?' asked Tory, turning her back on the

approach of Carla and her recent tormentor.

'Denzil Hallam—at least that's the name he goes by here on Airouna,' replied Magnus.

'You sound sceptical,' she observed.

'I am. He is, I believe, a fellow countryman of yours, but that is all that is known about him, even though he's been here about seven years.'

'What brought him here?'

'The story goes that he turned up here in a small sailing sloop which he claimed he'd sailed across the Atlantic single-handed. He was ragged, half-starved and had no money to speak of, yet by the end of a year he'd taken over the management of the small marina and yacht-chartering business which is in the bay. In return for a berth for his sloop he worked there when he first came, skippering yachts, his own included, which were hired by tourists to cruise about the islands. Under his management the business has grown and the fleet of charter yachts is now one of the largest in the islands; it attracts tourists from all over the place. Consequently Hallam is very popular with the Government's department of tourism, but I wouldn't trust him as far as I can see him.'

'Oh. Why not?'

'He has a ruthless way of doing things, drives a hard bargain. And then his reputation with women isn't very good. He's taken up with one or two young women since I've been here, then dropped them quite heartlessly, so I'm told.' Magnus glanced over her shoulder, looked slightly embarrassed and bent forward to whisper. 'I'll tell you more about him later.'

Tory turned. Carla and the dark man were very near.

'Hello, Hallam,' Magnus said with an obvious effort to be cordial. 'You look as if you've been living dangerously as usual. What happened?'

Denzil Hallam's thick eyebrows tilted mockingly, and from under the hard brim of the white-topped yachtsman's hat which now covered his dark hair, his eyes glinted with unkind mirth as he stopped to lean on his crutches and look at Tory. Then his glance drifted away from her to Magnus and his hard mouth curled scornfully at one corner.

'I was crewing on a friend's yacht up north last week. We were racing and were caught by the tail end of Hurricane Enid. The wind stood the yacht on her ear, and reducing sail on the foredeck was a slippery business. I got off pretty lightly with a few bruises and a sprained ankle,' he replied coolly.

'And are lucky to be alive to tell the tale, I suppose. I hear that Enid did a lot of damage on the east coast of the States,' said Magnus.

The hard green-flecked tawny eyes considered him for a moment, and then flicked back to Tory.

'I didn't know you had two daughters, Dr Jarrold,' said Denzil Hallam with a suave politeness which was belied by the wicked gleam in his eyes. Tory tightened her lips and looked away from him, only to see Carla's face crumple with laughter at the wild suggestion that she and Tory could be sisters.

'I haven't,' replied Magnus with a smile. 'This young lady is Tory Latham. She's a botanist and has to come to work at the Gardens under my direction.'

'A beautiful botanist.' The devil wasn't even trying to conceal his amusement at her expense now, and Tory felt herself trembling with an effort to appear unconcerned. 'I didn't realise that there was such a species, Doctor, and I congratulate you on your good taste,' he added outrageously. 'But Tory seems an odd sort of name for a woman. I've always thought it was the name of a political party.'

'It's short for Victoria,' snapped Tory, goaded beyond endurance by his mockery, then wished she had kept her mouth shut when he laughed outright.

'Oho, now I understand your lack of amusement back there on the ferryboat,' he scoffed. 'Your reaction was extremely Victorian.'

'What's this? Have you and Tory met already?' Magnus sounded sharp and anxious but before she could think up an answer to ease his mind Denzil Hallam had said lazily,

'Oh, we didn't just meet. We collided head-on, with extremely interesting results, wouldn't you say, Miss Latham?'

He was being deliberately provocative, paying her back for her unaccountable behaviour on the boat, and Tory was beginning to feel a little ill as she stood there under the hot sun. She was, she noticed, the only one not wearing a hat, for Carla had a pretty wide-brimmed affair perched on her thick bouncy hair, Instead of rising to the bait which Denzil Hallam had trailed with another sharp answer, she began to search in her canvas holdall for her hat and was relieved to hear Magnus say rather diffidently,

'Can we give you a lift, Hallam? As you know we pass the marina on our way to the Gardens.'

'No, thanks.' The answer was crisp and brought Tory more relief because to have had his company in a car would have been unbearable. 'I'm expecting Josh, and in fact I think I can hear the jeep coming now. It's been nice meeting you, Victoria Latham.' He paused, but when she did not look up or make any acknowledgement he added curtly, 'I expect I'll be seeing you around, Doctor. You too, Carla.'

He swung away on his crutches just as Tory settled her hat on her head.

'Denzil, wait!' Carla was after him at speed, catching up with him as a blue jeep screeched to a stop beside him.

'Carla, come back at once. We're going now,'

Magnus's command was quite ineffectual. 'Damn,' he added softly as he watched his daughter speaking to the tough piratical-looking man on crutches. He turned to Tory with an apologetic smile.

'You see what I mean? You see what I'm up against? A magnetic force which I imagine most women find hard to resist, to say nothing of a teenager like Carla. What did he mean about you and he colliding on the boat?'

'I walked into him, that's all,' replied Tory coolly. 'He tried to make capital out of the incident.'

'Mmm. That sounds like Hallam. But I mustn't keep you standing about in the hot sun any longer. You're looking a little pale, and I expect you're feeling tired after your long journey.'

More than tired, thought Tory; absolutely exhausted, washed out, because for some reason the excitement that had kept her going ever since she had received Magnus's letter had seeped away, leaving her feeling flat and disappointed.

He picked up her cases and led the way to a cream-coloured car. Magnus opened the boot and put her cases in it. As he closed it he glanced across to the jeep.

'Ha! As I thought, Hallam has no time to spare for Carla today, so she's coming back,' he said.

But apparently Denzil did have time to spare for Carla, for when the girl arrived, her shoulder-length hair bouncing against her bare tawny skin and her black eyes ablaze with excitement, she announced,

'I'm going with Denzil in the jeep.'

'No. I forbid it,' said Magnus sharply.

'Oh, don't be so mean, Daddy,' Carla wheedled. 'He says I can swim at the pool at the marina and he'll drive me home later.'

'No.' Magnus sounded thoroughly harassed and Tory racked her tired brain for some way of helping him.

'Why not?' Carla's full red lips pouted prettily.

'Because I don't want you to have anything to do with that man.'

'But why?' whined Carla.

'I've told you several times already. Now get in the car, and remember we have a guest who has come a long way and is feeling tired.'

Carla glanced at Tory. It was a truly female glance, unsmiling and critical; the glance of a woman taking the measure of another member of her sex and weighing up the competition, and it infuriated Tory even more than Denzil Hallam's bold raking glance of admiration had done.

'Is *your* father stuffy about your relationship with other men?' asked Carla.

The question disconcerted Tory. Carla was appealing to her as a contemporary, possibly hoping to enlist her as an ally against a member of the older generation, namely Magnus, whom his daughter saw as a stuffy, fussy father yet whom Tory regarded as a much respected and admired friend.

'I don't think I've ever heard my father express an opinion on the subject,' she replied evasively.

Again Carla's dark eyes measured her and dismissed her.

'Oh, I can see you're going to be no help to me at all. You're on his side,' she said, jerking her head in Magnus's direction just as the sound of the jeep's engine being revved caused her to whirl round. As the vehicle moved off in the direction of the square, Carla let out a wail of frustration and stamped her foot.

'Now look what's happened! And it's all your fault,' she cried, turning accusingly to her father, who looked very surprised by her attack. 'If I hadn't had to come and ask you if I could go I'd be on my way by now. He's gone without me.'

'And saved me a lot of trouble,' said Magnus dryly. 'Not that I ever want to be in debt to that doubtful character. Get in the back of the car, Carla, and you sit in front with me, Tory, and we'll be going too.'

The atmosphere inside the car was stifling because it had been parked in the full glare of the sun. The vinyl-covered seats had become over-heated so that when she sat down Tory almost jumped up again, as even through the stuff of her dress her thighs felt as if they had been seared. And when she grasped the chromium door-handle to pull the door shut she gasped, for it was like taking hold of a naked flame.

'You'll find many reminders of England in this part of the town,' said Magnus chattily as he drove through the shady square and down the main street. 'Most of the old shops and horses are built of bricks which were brought over as a ballast in the schooners which came to pick up sugar in the eighteenth century.'

Looking out, Tory saw arcades with rounded arches casting deep shade over sidewalks which had very high curbs and deep gutters. Where there wasn't any shade sunlight gilded white paint and glinted on plain sash windows edged with blue or red louvred shutters. Purple bougainvillaea and scarlet creeping geraniums cascaded over the sides of window boxes, vivid splashes of colour against white wood or black ironwork.

Magnus braked suddenly and she looked through the windscreen to see three shapely dark-skinned women, wearing printed cotton shifts and carrying baskets of goods balanced on their turbanned heads, drift gracefully across the road.

'There isn't much vehicular traffic on the island, so the local people walk back and forth just as they like,' explained Magnus with a smile. 'I expect those three have been to the market. It's held in a hall in a street parallel to this one, and you have to be there early if you want to buy a goat or a chicken, fresh fruit, or perhaps a length of printed cotton. Look over to the left—there's something else which is very English. The Anglican Cathedral.'

It was a pretty church with a castellated square tower and it was set in a leafy garden. Tory had a glimpse of a wide pathway shaded by graceful almond trees leading up to a Georgian portico. On either side of the entrance was a row of oblong, fan-topped windows set into brick walls the white paint of which had been washed away here and there so that the original red colour of the brick showed through in a patchwork effect.

'I didn't realise that poinsettia could grow so big,' exclaimed Tory, recognising the shaggy shape of leaves on the bushes crowding one corner of the walled garden. 'And those big trees over there are Royal Poinciana, aren't they?'

'*Delonix regia*,' said Magnus, slanting a smile in her direction. 'You're quite right. I suppose you think of poinsettia as small plants in pots cultivated for Christmas and not as huge ornamental shrubs as they are here. That particular garden was established by the first Director of the Botanical Gardens, as long ago as 1760.'

'He was Sir Jeffrey Downs,' she put in.

'Right again. Anyone can tell, Miss Latham, that you specialised in horticultural science,' he teased, and she felt a warm glow spread through her to disperse the greyness of disappointment. She was with Magnus again and they were talking their language, the language of botanists who were steeped in their own particular branch of the science. It was a common interest which had brought them together in the first place, which had brought them together now and which would keep them together in the future, Tory hoped.

They left the town behind and followed a road which was little more than a winding lane through the banana bush. Here and there wooden huts with steeply sloping roofs of thatch squatted among the trees. Washing pegged to lines strung between the trunks of banana palms and fluttering in the steady breeze indicated that the huts were inhabited. On a clearing of sunbaked earth some barefooted black boys were playing cricket.

The road dipped down a hill, then wound close to a beach of pale sand that curved beside shimmering turquoise water under the shade of leaning coconut palms. Beyond the beach Tory had a glimpse of the tall masts of sailing boats and the shining white super-structures of many motor cruisers tied up at pontoons, and then the view was screened by sea-grape trees and thick casuarinas enclosed by a white fence that edged the road. A large sign appeared at the wayside. It advertised that a few yards ahead they would reach the entrance to the Blue Horizons Marina, where yachts and cruisers of all kinds and sizes could be chartered by the hour, the day or the week.

'Daddy, please let me off at the gate of the marina so I can go to the pool. I'm longing to swim.' Carla broke the smouldering silence in which she had sat all the way from the harbour.

'You can swim from the beach at home,' replied Magnus.

'But it's so far from the house. It takes ages to walk there, and it's not the same. There's no one there. It isn't any fun,' moaned Carla. 'Daddy, please!'

'No. I'm certainly not going back on my word and letting you out to go and hang around a man with a reputation like Hallam's,' said Magnus irritably.

'I don't hang around him,' protested Carla hotly.

'Yes, you do. Now please be quiet.'

Carla slumped back against the back of her seat

muttering to herself, and Tory gave Magnus a wary sidelong glance. The man who had lectured to her at university had never been irritable, nor had he ever spoken sharply. Now he was frowning and there was a pinched look about his face which destroyed the impression he usually gave of charming boyishness and good humour.

She looked away from him quickly, just in time to see the entrance to the marina; a wide driveway of sandy gravel glittering in the bright sunlight. A blue jeep was parked in front of a modern two-storey office-like building and beyond that were the enticing boats, tied up in orderly rows between floating grey pontoons which stretched across the corner of the bay.

'Not far now,' said Magnus, the sharpness gone from his voice. 'Unfortunately, from my point of view that is, Hallam is our nearest neighbour. The distance from the gates of the marina to the gates of the Botanical Gardens is five miles, but if you come over that hill through the rain forest it's only a mile and a half.'

The road climbed in a series of bends. It topped a hill and there below them lay a green valley caught between two ridges of low hills. Another series of bends took them down into a valley where the road straightened beside a sturdy grey stone wall in front of which bright red hibiscus flowers clustered. The wall ended at an opening marked by square stone gateposts surmounted by stone balls.

Magnus turned the car through the opening into a landscaped park which made Tory gasp with delight. As they drove along the smooth driveway she sat in silence, marvelling at the careful planning and planting which had been done in the past to produce such attractive contrasts of foliage and blossom.

Round a shimmering blue-reflecting pond they drove, where two white swans sailed in state. Delicate white poinsettia, known as Snow Pillow because of the likeness of its blossom to a froth of drifting snow-flakes, drooped over the pool. Yellow spikes of the candle bush, dark red tails of the chenille plant, golden trumpets of allamanda, flush-pink beaks of the Bird of Paradise flower, they were all there growing naturally, their colours contrasting and sometimes clashing, set off by the green spikes of Spanish Bayonet and the thick heart-shaped leaves of anthurium.

Leaving the pool, the driveway crossed green lawns shaded by giant tulip trees and led the way to an elegant Georgian house. Four white pillars supported its portico over a panelled front door which had a spider-web window above it. Wide shallow steps led up to the porch, and at either end of each step was a large pottery jar foaming with purple bougainvillaea, red begonias and delicate pink spray orchids.

Magnus had hardly braked when Carla was out of the car. Banging the door closed, she raced away up the steps and disappeared into the house.

'Well, here we are,' said Magnus, 'This is home. The director's house built for the Sir Jeffrey you mentioned earlier. As you can see, it's far too big for Carla and me, so I'm glad you're going to occupy one of the rooms. I was unable to find any alternative accommodation for you. All the bungalows provided for the botanists and gardeners are full and any other accommodation is in Port Anne eight miles away. I expect you'll be glad to get indoors and have a wash and change your clothing.'

'Yes, I shall. I don't think I've ever felt so sticky with heat before.'

'It'll take you a while to become acclimatised, and I think that right now you should have a rest. We can talk later when the sun goes down. There's so much I have to tell you, Tory, about my plans for the book.'

They went up the wide shallow steps, through the

door into a high-ceilinged hallway where a small black woman with frizzy grey hair snatched back into a tight knob on top of her head was waiting for them. Magnus introduced her as Mrs Dunnet, the housekeeper. A dark-skinned smiling boy wearing spotless white shorts and shirt appeared, and at an instruction from Mrs Dunnet he picked up Tory's cases and went off up the wide central staircase.

With Mrs Dunnet, Tory followed the boy up the un-carpeted shining stairs to a wooden gallery which ran round the upper part of the hall. They went past several closed doors to a door which was open, and entered a lovely big room which had pale sea-green walls, white woodwork and turquoise-coloured drapes at two long windows opening on to tiny balconies.

The door of the room closed as Mrs Dunnet and the boy left, and alone at last Tory kicked off her white shoes, peeled off the nylon tights which she should never have worn on such a hot day, and lay down on the silken turquoise bed.

Hands under her head, she stared at the ceiling. Its plasterwork was intricately carved with leaves and flowers and could have been in a similar house in England.

But it was here on this island, known as the Isle of the Blest, and so was she. England was far away and so were her family, her parents, her brother George and her sister Robina. Both her mother and her brother had been against this adventure of hers and she knew why they had been. They both thought she was making a fool of herself over a man old enough to be her father.

'What's this Magnus Jarrold like?' George had asked when she told him of the job Magnus had offered her.

'Oh, about forty-five, looks younger, about six feet one, slightly built, reddish hair, blue eyes ...'

'Wears glasses, has knobbly knees,' George had interrupted her jeeringly. 'I don't mean what does he look like, I mean what makes him tick for you? You're pretty keen on him, aren't you?'

'Am I?' Tory had tried to retort lightly.

'You can't fool me,' had replied the young man who for most of his twenty years had been her friend, tormentor and confidant. 'You should have seen yourself light up over that letter. I don't think I've seen you so excited since you learnt you'd won a scholarship to university.'

'Well, wouldn't you be excited if you'd been offered an opportunity to go and work on a tropical island with a man you admire, and who happens to be brilliant in his own field of science?' she had defended herself.

'Of course I'd be glad, but I doubt if I'd blush over it,' George had scoffed. 'You're not going because of the job. You're going because you've got a crush on Magnus Jarrold.'

'I haven't. I'm too old for crushes,' she had denied hotly. 'Honestly, George, I'd thought better of you. Fancy jumping to a conclusion like that before studying the facts!'

'Seems to me I'm close to the mark,' he had retorted with a grin. 'And there's a trend lately, isn't there, for young women to fall for men old enough to be their fathers?'

'Magnus isn't . . .' she had begun, and stopped to stare at him as she did a rapid mental calculation. 'Magnus is exactly twenty-two years older than I am,' she had admitted reluctantly.

'You see?' George had taunted smugly.

Her mother's approach had been more serious and practical.

'The Caribbean is such a long way from here. Supposing you're ill while you're out there?' she had said.

'I've been away from home before, to university, and

24

managed quite well, and I've held down a job here for a year. Honestly, Mother, the way you're talking you'd think I was still a child unable to manage my own affairs,' Tory had said,

Pamela Latham had given her a shrewd glance and had said quietly,

'That's the trouble. In some ways I don't think you are able to manage a certain sort of affair.'

'What do you mean?' Tory had demanded.

'I mean, love, that you're a lovely stubborn woman who is strangely innocent for this day and age, the result, I think, of being more interested in plants than in people. You know next to nothing about this man, yet you're going quite happily to live in his house.'

'I do know something about him! I know he's clever and kind, a brilliant teacher of his own subject who has already taught me a great deal about botany ...'

'Is he married?' Pamela's quiet determined question had stopped Tory short in her eulogy of Magnus's finer points of character.

'I ... I don't know,' she had mumbled. 'He doesn't seem to be married.'

'There you are,' said the worldly-wise Pamela, who worked as a secretary to the headmaster of a big comprehensive high school nearby. 'You know nothing about him.'

'I know all that matters,' Tory had argued stubbornly. 'Anyway, I don't much care if he is married. I'm going to Airouna to work for him. It's a chance I can't afford to miss, and you can't stop me from going.'

'I know I can't,' Pamela had sighed. 'I wouldn't mind, only I know you and that blind stubborn faith you have in any person who catches your fancy. I can only hope you don't get hurt and that your knight in shining armour doesn't turn out to have feet of clay.'

Tory blinked. The ornate carving of the plaster ceiling had blurred suddenly. She touched her eyes and found to her surprise that they were full of tears. How right her mother had been! Magnus was, or had been, married. Carla was proof of that.

Yet he had never told her. It wasn't as if he hadn't had plenty of opportunities to tell her. They had spent many hours together in the university laboratory when he had been a full-time assistant professor; hovering over microscopes, studying specimens and comparing their observations, conducting experiments on plant genetics. He had even taken her out to tea several times to a dark-beamed, low-ceilinged teashop near the university where the cakes and scones had been home-made.

And it was on the basis of those hours spent talking together about the science in which they were both interested that Tory had formed her attachment to him. When he had left to take up the position of director of the Airounian Botanical Gardens she had been most unhappy, and when he had returned during her final term to give some talks to the graduating students about the work he was doing she had been delighted. When he had singled her out and asked her if she would consider coming to Airouna to work for him and help him with the book he was compiling about plants of the Caribbean, it had seemed to her that life could offer her nothing more wonderful.

So she had come. And now she was lying there thinking how true was the saying that it is better to travel hopefully than to arrive, for although the island and its setting were far more beautiful than she had ever dreamed, and although Magnus was just the same, her arrival had been spoilt by the shock of meeting Carla and the realisation that somewhere in this house there might be a woman whom she had yet to meet—Mrs Magnus Jarrold.

CHAPTER TWO

IMPATIENT with her thoughts, Tory jack-knifed into a sitting position. Being an essentially practical person with a fairly serene outlook on life, she did not go in much for introspection; she preferred action to sitting around moping. Her recent self-indulgence in a few tears had been merely the result of being overtired. The fatigue produced by travelling a long way in a short time had lowered her spirits and robbed her temporarily of her usual resilience.

But she was bouncing back. What did she care if Magnus had a wife? She could still work for him and worship from a distance, enjoy a spiritual and purely platonic relationship with him. After all, he had never shown any indication that he had ever wanted any other sort of relationship with her. And if there was a Mrs Jarrold it would be better if she prepared herself to meet her by unpacking her clothing and hanging it up in the big walk-in closet, and then finding out what washing facilities the house provided.

Springing off the bed, Tory started to unlock her cases. It took her the best part of half an hour to unpack and arrange her clothing satisfactorily. That done, she went in search of a bathroom and found to her delight that she had a private one opening off the room. It was very modern, with green tiles and a bath-tub into which she had to step down. It didn't, however, live up to its promise, for the water-pressure was temperamental. Sometimes water gushed madly from the tap, sometimes there was none at all. The temperature of it also seemed to be uncontrollable and it either scalded her or chilled her, so that after several unsuccessful attempts to have a shower she decided it would be safer in future to have a complete bath.

Eventually, clean and refreshed, her blonde hair smooth and shining, and her simple evening gown of delphinium blue flattering her long shapely figure, Tory went downstairs to face up to the reality of Magnus's wife.

But when she found him on the terrace at the back of the house, to which she had been directed by Mrs Dunnet, he was alone, sitting in a chair made from white cane and watching the crimson-flushed western sky from which the sun had slipped suddenly behind a dark blue ridge of hills. When he saw her he stood up punctiliously and gestured to another chair of white cane.

'Do sit down, Tory—I'm afraid Carla has the sulks and won't come down for dinner. Let me help you to some of Mrs Dunnet's fruit punch. It makes an excellent sundowner.'

He ladled some golden liquid from a huge cut-glass bowl, which was set on a small wrought iron table, into a tall glass, added ice cubes from a silver bucket and decorated the edge of the glass with a slice of orange.

He handed her the glass, took his seat and raised his own glass in a toast.

'Here's to a splendid new partnership, you and me,' he said brightly. 'I feel sure our work together during the next few months is going to be valuable and productive. What do you think of your room?'

'It seems very comfortable and elegant, though I had one or two problems with the water in the bathroom,' she said, and took a sip of her drink. It was delicious, a blending of pineapple with citrus fruits and another new flavour which she could not recognise.

'It's coconut juice,' said Magnus softly. He had been watching her drink and had read the expression of

28

puzzlement on her open fair face. 'It's the best drink in the islands for slaking the thirst. About the water—I'm afraid it's a problem we have to live with. I've known the pressure to be down to nil even while a tropical downpour has been hissing and steaming outside. Electricity is temperamental too and the supply can fail several times in one week. But I think you'll find the advantages of living here outweigh the disadvantages. This is a nice island with good people. You'll find the food good too, Mrs Dunnet is an excellent cook. Her breadfruit soufflés are out of this world for lightness and tastiness.'

So far no word about his wife. It looked as if she would have to ask him outright.

'Magnus, I ... I ... meeting Carla was a shock. I didn't know you were ... are ... had been married.' It came out garbled, but at least it was said.

'Mmm.' He studied the contents of his glass and frowned. Light was fading rapidly from the sky but she could see he was worried. 'Yes, well ... er ... it isn't one of the subjects one normally discusses with students in a seminar,' he said slowly.

The dart found its target. Tory felt the shock of pain as she realised that was all she had ever been to him— a student from one of his seminars.

'Is she ... your wife here?' she managed to say.

'No, she's ...' He broke off to take a long pull at his drink, draining the glass, and set it down empty on the table. Studying his averted face, Tory decided it pained him to talk of his wife because she was no longer alive, and at once she felt an easing of her own small pain.

'Please don't say any more,' she said in a low voice, leaning forward. 'I think I understand.'

Magnus turned to look at her. The fast-falling tropical dusk was all about them, but in the glow of yellow light which came from lamps which had been lit in the room behind the terrace she saw him smile at her.

'That's a relief,' he murmured, and leaned forward too to take her free hand in both of his. 'But then I've always thought you were a most understanding person, older than your years, and that's why I'm going to ask you to help me with Carla. She's been at a boarding school in England for the past five years, but she finished there last June and came here, and I don't know what to do with her. Since she arrived she's been in one scrape after another.'

He heaved a weary sigh and Tory's heart contracted with compassion. How she longed to ease his anxiety, to be of help to him! 'Quite frankly, Tory,' he continued diffidently, 'I'm not much of a parent. I get too engrossed in my work. When it comes to coping with teenage girls I haven't a clue what to do. She really needs more guidance than I can give her.'

'What do you think I can do to help?' said Tory recklessly, once more committing herself wholeheartedly to this man who seemed so much in need of her strength and abilities.

'I'm not really sure,' he said with a self-deprecating laugh. 'I was hoping you'd know what to do. You could perhaps give her some advice in a sisterly way, tell her perhaps how easy it is for a girl of her vulnerable age to be led astray by an older, more experienced man like Hallam.'

Tory sat very still, her hand caught between both of his. The irony of the situation did not escape her. Here was Magnus appealing to her to guide his daughter away from the path which she was treading herself, and apparently quite oblivious to the fact that she was attracted to him, a man much older than herself, in the same way that Carla was attracted to Denzil Hallam.

There's a trend lately for young women to fall for men old enough to be their fathers. Her brother

George's mocking statement flashed into her mind, and withdrawing her hand from Magnus's clasp she leaned back in her chair to take another sip of her drink.

'You're very quiet,' remarked Magnus. 'Have I asked too much of you? I realise that it's a presumption on my part to ask you to keep an eye on Carla when you've come here to do work which you've been trained to do, but I'd be very grateful if you would. Perhaps you could suggest some form of training she might take? She doesn't seem to have any ideas of what she wants to do with her life. As far as I can make out all she's interested in is having *fun*, and she doesn't seem to be able to have it anywhere else on the island but at Hallam's marina. And the worst part of it all is that he doesn't hesitate to encourage her to go there.'

'No, you haven't asked too much. I'll do what I can,' Tory answered quickly, noting the bitter, discouraged note which had crept into his voice. 'But have you ever had a word with Mr Hallam yourself about Carla going there? Maybe if you approached him and told him how you feel about it he would stop encouraging her.'

'I've thought of doing that, but each time I've discarded the idea.'

'Why?' Tory could scarcely believe her ears. For a father to go and speak his mind to someone whom he thought was having a bad influence on his child seemed the correct action to take to her way of thinking.

'You've met the man, briefly I know,' responded Magnus, 'but you've some idea of what he's like, so you can imagine how he would react if I went to him and said: "Please don't encourage my daughter to come to your marina any more." Why, he'd laugh in my face.'

Tory stared at him in amazement. At shaft of golden light from the room behind illuminated his face quite clearly, and for the first time she saw weakness there and not sensitivity. Then Magnus's slightly snub nose, protuberant blue eyes and clean-shaven rounded chin were obliterated as she had a sudden inward vision of a lean, dark face in which the eyes danced with wicked humour and the wide mouth had a twist of scorn to it. Yes, one blast of Denzil Hallam's mockery would shrivel Magnus.

But *she* wouldn't be shrivelled! She was made of stronger stuff than this highly intelligent man and she could use her strength to bolster him. In fact the idea of going to cross swords with the pirate who managed the marina appealed to her. He had bested her at their first meeting by making her feel that she had over-reacted to what he had insisted had been an attempt to befriend her. He had made her appear to be narrow-minded and ungenerous, and by doing so had roused her hostility so that she found herself looking for a chance to get her own back.

'Perhaps I could go and see him and ask him not to encourage Carla to visit him,' she murmured.

'Good heavens, no!' exclaimed Magnus. 'I couldn't let you put yourself into such a position.'

'But it might work. It's possible that he doesn't realise how anxious you are about Carla,' she argued.

'And do you think he would really care if he did realise it?' he challenged. 'Oh no, my dear, Hallam isn't the sort to consider anyone else's feelings. He's tough, and is only to be approached as a last resort if we find nothing you do or say has any effect on Carla's behaviour. And now let's go and have some dinner and forget about such problems. I want to tell you what your appointment as an assistant botanist in charge of horticulture is going to involve.'

It took Tory almost a month to become acclimatised and adjusted to the routine of work. During those four weeks she travelled by car from one end of the island to the other. First she went by the windward highway where low cliffs dropped sheer to beaches of black sand, past terraces planted with sugar-cane and fields where cattle grazed as far as the slopes of the wicked volcanic mountain that lurked among white clouds. Another time she went by the leeward highway, which swung and twisted through forest-covered crags and banana plantations, along a coast indented with sheltered bays, through sleepy fishing villages where nets were set out to dry, and again reached the foot of the mountain.

The journeys were made with Magnus and were part of his plan to introduce her to village communities as someone who could come when required to give talks, complete with a coloured film, on how they could make their small gardens more productive and attractive.

At the Botanical Gardens themselves, she was kept busy writing up simple pamphlets giving information about plants that could be grown in small gardens, as well as setting up experiments in cross-breeding to develop new pest-resistant species of food-producing plants such as maize. In her spare time she helped Magnus with his book.

With all this activity Tory did not have much time to show an interest in Carla, but she did try, only to have her attempts met by blank stares, sulky silences or rude remarks. She said nothing of his daughter's un-co-operative behaviour to Magnus because she was afraid he might take the girl to task, and Carla would then consider her a tell-tale, and any chance of winning her confidence would be lost entirely.

She was beginning to think that perhaps the girl had given up going to the marina when a chance meeting with Carla in the early hours one morning disillusioned her. She had woken for some reason and had been un-able to go to sleep again. Deciding she might settle if she read a while, she went downstairs to Magnus's study to select a novel from the bookcase. She had just turned out the light in the study and was about to cross the moonlit hall when the sound of the front door being pushed open slowly made her pause. The door swung wider and a figure entered stealthily, turning to close the door gently.

Recognising Carla's short slight figure, Tory stepped to the light switch and clicked it on.

'And where have you been until now?' she asked.

Carla whirled round. She was dressed in blue cotton pants and a simple cotton T-shirt; sparks of light glittered on the glossiness of her black hair. After an initial flash of surprise her dark eyes became opaque and sullen. Her full red lips pursed in a stubborn pout.

'Why should I tell you? You've no authority over me,' she challenged.

'Maybe I haven't, but I can still be interested in what you're doing and why you're doing it,' replied Tory calmly. 'Don't you think it's a little strange that I should find you returning to the house at this hour of the morning, when you're supposed to be in bed?'

'I suppose you're going to tell my father?' demanded Carla.

'Not necessarily. Carla, how many times have you done this, told him you were going to bed and then crept out of the house to return this late?'

'Not many. Only when there's been a party.'

'What sort of party? Where?'

'At the marina. Sometimes people who charter yachts give parties when they return from a cruise, before they fly back to the States.'

'And are you invited to them?'

'Not exactly ... but if I'm there and I hang around long enough, Denzil says why don't I stay, so I stay.'

Tory chewed her lower lip as she searched for a way

to tell the girl that she shouldn't do everything which the manager of the marina suggested.

'Look, Carla, what you're doing isn't right, can't you see that?' she began.

'What's wrong about it?'

'You're deceiving your father for a start.'

'So what?' The girl shrugged her shoulders. 'You know very well that if I asked his permission he'd say no, so I go without asking.'

Tory swallowed hard. Dealing with this girl was difficult. She seemed to be hard all the way through.

'You should be more careful,' she said, 'you shouldn't do everything a man like Denzil Hallam suggests. He could take advantage of you.'

Carla grinned suddenly, a knowing incorrigible grin.

'I wish he would,' she retorted.

'You don't mean that,' snapped Tory, feeling a little shocked by the girl's outspokenness.

'Yes, I do.'

'But he's so much older than you,' protested Tory.

'He's thirty-four! That's twice my age. How much older than you is my father? About the same, I'd guess, so you're a fine one to be handing out advice like that to me, aren't you?'

It seemed to Tory that the safe little world in which she had been living for the past month, the world of microscopes, gardens and botanical terms had come tumbling down about her ears, leaving her exposed to criticism and mockery.

'What do you mean?' she gasped weakly.

'You think I'm sweet on Denzil,' said Carla harshly. 'Well, I am, because he's fun to be with as well as being big and strong and understanding.' The harsh voice quivered a little and almost broke. Carla bit her lip to control whatever emotion had bubbled up and then continued on a lower fiercer note. 'But I'm not half as sweet on him as you are on my father. I think it's time you took your own advice, Miss High and Mighty Latham, before *you're* taken advantage of!'

Her burst of emotion over, Carla turned and went running up the stairs, reckless of the noise she made on the uncarpeted wooden treads. Down a passage she pounded, the door to her room crashed open and then crashed shut again, and there was silence.

More than disturbed by the girl's outburst, Tory returned to her bedroom and lay down on the bed. She tried to read but could not concentrate. Carla's words were ringing in her ears. They had been flung at her, she realised, because the girl had resented the advice which had been offered and had seized the nearest weapon to hand and used it clumsily but effectively. For although Tory knew there wasn't the slightest possibility of Magnus taking advantage of her in the way she had suggested, though Denzil Hallam might take advantage of Carla or any other woman who showed an interest in him, it was the fact that Carla had noticed Tory's liking for her father which was most disturbing. If she had noticed, others must have noticed too.

Tory sighed, laid the book on the bedside table and clicked off the light. Settling again under the single sheet which was all she had found she needed as a covering during the warm nights, she admitted ruefully to herself that she was making a mess of trying to help Magnus cope with his daughter. There seemed to be no way for her to reach the girl, who possessed very little of Magnus's sensitivity.

Carla must be like her mother, not only physically but in other ways too—and possibly the fact that the girl was motherless and had spent all those years in a girl's boarding school, where she had learned to fend for herself, had made her hard and rebellious.

Next day Magnus announced that he was going to

the island of Martinique for a few days at the invitation of the Director of the Botanical Gardens there.

'I've told Carla and she's promised she'll behave herself,' he said. 'How are you and she getting on together?'

Obviously he hadn't noticed the strained relations between herself and Carla at the meal table, and it occurred to Tory with a sudden flash of insight that Magnus didn't notice anything he didn't like because he had the mentality of an ostrich, burying his head and ignoring the unpleasant aspects of life.

In the next moment she rejected this startling observation, about someone whom she had always regarded as admirable, as unkind and unworthy of her.

'Not as well as I'd like,' she replied. 'Would you mind if I asked you a personal question about your wife?'

'About Rita?' His voice lilted with surprise. 'No, I don't. Go ahead.'

'Is Carla like her?'

'She has, of course, Rita's colouring, but she's not as beautiful,' he replied quietly.

'And in temperament?'

He didn't reply at once, and in the silence which lay between them she could hear the night song of frogs and the rustle of leaves stirred by the wind coming from the garden through the open windows.

Magnus spoke very slowly, as if it gave him pain to speak of his wife.

'Yes, in temperament too. That's why I'm worried about the child, and about her infatuation with Hallam. I'm so afraid she might be hurt by him and then cast off. Rita was hurt in that way once. You see, Tory, when I first met her she was married to the most awful man who had treated her unkindly and then deserted her.'

'Oh, I see,' she whispered. 'Thank you for telling me.'

She took the information to bed with her and pondered over it before she slept. It reinforced her opinion of Magnus as the sort of person to whom a woman who was unhappy might turn, and of whom the same woman might take advantage, using his pity to trap him into marriage with her.

He left the next day, but it wasn't until he had been gone for three days that Tory realised she had hardly seen Carla and was forced to ask Mrs Dunnet if she knew anything of the girl's whereabouts.

'Dat girl no good,' stated the little woman, rolling her big brown eyes. 'She ain't been home since yesterday.'

'Do you have any idea where she's gone?'

'I reckon she spent de night down at dat marina, miss.'

'Then I shall go there at once and bring her back,' said Tory determinedly. The time had come for her to use the last resort, to go and beard Denzil Hallam in his den and tell him to stop encouraging Carla to visit him.

She went in the cream car which Magnus allowed her to use. When she turned into the entrance of the marina she found several cars parked in a yard beside the office building. The blue jeep was there too.

But as soon as she saw the masts of the sailing boats nostalgia claimed Tory. She had to go and look at them. It was almost two months since she had last gone sailing with George in their racing dinghy, but it wasn't until now that she realised how much she had missed the activity of sailing and messing about in boats.

Up and down the pontoons she wandered, pausing every so often to stare in amazement at the forceful thrusting lines of a new fibreglass cruiser or to admire the graceful sweep of the bow of an old wooden schooner. The hot sun struck down at her fair head and she pulled on her sunhat. She was wearing a sleeveless red and white striped cotton sweater and crisp white slacks, but wished she had taken time to change into a sundress which would have been cooler.

As she reached the last pontoon she found some small fibreglass dinghies tied up. They had slim glinting masts and looked fast and lively. She felt a sudden urge to be in one of them, skimming over the glittering blue water of the bay, feeling the wind lift her hair and the salt spray sting her skin ...

'So I wasn't mistaken, the beautiful botanist has condescended to pay us a visit,' said a voice behind her, and she turned to find Denzil Hallam there.

Without crutches, his deeply tanned muscular legs revealed by brief well-tailored brown shorts, a cream shirt taut across his shoulders and open almost to the waist for coolness, he looked clean and efficient. From beneath the tilted brim of his white-topped yachting cap his hard eyes regarded her unsmilingly. His hostility seemed tangible, something which reached out and touched her, warning Tory to go carefully.

'Why have you come?' he asked coldly.

'I was admiring the dinghies,' she replied evasively. It was not the time to approach the subject of Carla. She would have to establish some kind of communication with him before she dared ask him where the girl was. 'Do you hire them out?'

'Yes, for four beewee dollars an hour,' he replied coolly. She knew now that 'beewee' was an island colloquialism for British West Indian currency. 'But I hire them only to people who have some idea of how to sail,' he added.

'I've been sailing and crewing in dinghies for almost as long as I can remember,' she said.

39

'Those would be two-sail jobs, these are single-handed craft. You'd capsize one in a breeze like this before you'd got under way,' he jeered.

'No, I wouldn't,' she retorted, 'and if you don't believe me, why don't you let me hire one and show you I can sail?'

He stared at her for a moment with narrowed eyes, then shrugged his shoulders.

'Okay. I'll get someone to fetch the sail and rig it,' he said, and half turned to go.

'And you'll watch from dry land, I suppose.' Her voice rang out in challenge. 'Oh no, that isn't good enough. I'll race you out to that orange marker buoy and back again, and I bet you'll find I'm just as good a sailor as you are.'

He swung slowly round to face her and again his hard narrowed gaze assessed her.

'So you like playing with fire, do you, Victoria?' he scoffed softly. 'And I've never been able to resist a challenge. All right, I'll take you on for the hire of the dinghy. But I'm warning you you're going to get wet. Will those elegant pants of yours stand up to salt water, or could you use a pair of shorts?'

Excited suddenly because he had responded to her challenge, Tory glanced down at her white slacks. It would be a shame to spoil them.

'Do you have any shorts that will fit me?' she asked.

'Sure. My girl-friends are always leaving their clothes behind. I suppose they think it gives them a good excuse to come back and see me again,' he drawled provocatively. 'There's a changing room in the office building. Go there and I'll bring you a pair.'

The shorts were really cut-off jeans, faded blue and frayed at the edges, but they fitted perfectly. Denzil Hallam had a good eye and had sized up her measurements fairly accurately, Tory thought with a grimace of distaste. How much she had disliked his reference to girl-friends who left their clothing behind after visiting him! It hinted that they stayed overnight with him. If she hadn't been so keen to sail she would never have agreed to wear clothing that belonged to a woman who had possibly shared his bed.

She found him waiting for her on the pontoon where the dinghies were tied up, talking to a huge black man whom he introduced as Josh and who acknowledged her in the usual friendly island way.

Denzil had also changed his clothes and was wearing battered-looking jean shorts and a thin short-sleeved cotton T-shirt. Both jeans and shorts emphasised the sturdy muscularity of his physique. He did not have the height of the other man, but once again Tory had the impression of immovable rock-like strength.

His glance went to the shorts she was wearing, then travelled insolently down her long bare legs, which had acquired an attractive golden tan since she had come to the island.

'The shorts seem to be a good fit,' he drawled, his glance coming up to meet her furious glare. 'What about shoes?'

'I'll sail in bare feet.'

'Okay. Now about the start of the race—you see that big motor cruiser on a mooring out there? Well, it's in line with the flagpole at the end of this pontoon, so we'll make that the starting line. Josh will fire a gun for the start, and for whoever finishes across the line the first. Which dinghy would you like?'

Two had been rigged and their shimmering terylene sails were flapping idly. Tory chose the yellow one and stepped down into it. The single sail was loose-footed and not attached to a boom. The dagger board was already down and she gave it a practice pull to see if she could get it up easily. Glancing up at Josh, she indicated that she was ready to go. He untied the boat and pushed it off.

Grabbing the tiller and winding the mainsheet round her other hand so that she could pull in the sail, Tory steered for the starting line, aware that Denzil's boat, a blue one, was still tied up. Wind filled the sail, the little boat heeled slightly and she automatically placed her weight on the side-deck so that she was ready to lean out. The wind increased in strength and the boat heeled more. She leaned right out, still steering with the tiller and still holding the mainsheet, and tucked her feet under the straps made from woven nylon which were attached to the bottom of the boat, to prevent her from falling out if she leaned too far.

Boom! The gun went off and she was across the starting line first. Looking up at her sail she saw the shadow of another sail beginning to move across it; Denzil was catching up on her. She looked round and saw the sharp pointed bow of his boat edging up. He was trying to overtake her by stealing the wind from her sail.

Quickly she pushed the tiller away from her. Her boat changed direction, moving towards his. Just as her sail began to flap because it was too close to the eye of the wind, she pulled the tiller towards her, the sail filled again and the little boat danced on its way.

Twice Denzil tried to pass her again in the same way and twice she prevented him from doing so. After the failure of his third attempt he changed his tactics, went on to the other tack and sailed away from her.

Tory knew he would have to tack again to reach the orange buoy, and so would she. Then they would be on converging courses and he would have right of way, but if she could sail faster than he, she could pass ahead of him.

Determined to do that, she tautened her sail and

leaned out as far as she could, knowing that the boat would go faster if it was not allowed to heel over too much. The boat bounced over the waves. Spray came up over the bow to soak her, but she didn't care because she was too exhilarated by the duel of wits and skill.

The round orange marker buoy bobbed like a ball on the heaving water. Tory took a quick glance under her sail, heard a voice roar 'starboard!' as the other boat came directly towards her, and knew a kick of satisfaction as she sailed blithely in front of him with a few yards to spare.

Immediately she went about, sailed straight for the buoy and was round it and on her way back to the finishing line, her sail full and bellying, only to find that the other boat was right beside her and was actually pulling ahead.

For the next few minutes she used every trick she could think of to get her boat to sail faster, pulling the sail in and then letting it out again, bringing the dagger board right up so that the boat could skim over the water, and eventually it seemed to her that her lighter weight was beginning to tell as she kept level with the blue boat.

Side by side the two boats seemed to fly over the water, their bows sending up spray. Tory made one more effort to go faster, and the little boat responded. Its bow came up as it rode on the crest of a wave across the finishing line.

Thrilled by the excitement of the close finish, Tory eased down the dagger board and pulled in her sail a little to change course for the approach to the pontoon. The sail filled with wind and the boat heeled so that she had to sit far out to keep it upright. She looked over her shoulder to see where the blue boat was, forgetting that she would soon be sheltered. Her sail emptied of wind suddenly and the boat, weighed down by her weight on the windward side, capsized the wrong way, dumping her in the warm silken water.

As the sail came towards her threatening to blanket her she kicked out vigorously and swam round the stern of the boat. Seeing the dagger board sticking out from the exposed bottom of the boat, like a fin on a fish, she grabbed it and pulled it down, then managed to stand on it. From that position she was able to grasp the rim of the boat and pull it upright.

Slowly the mast and sail came up. A quick wriggle and she was over the side and back in the boat. Grabbing mainsheet and tiller, her feet in the water which was swilling about in the bottom of the boat, she steered towards the side of the pontoon.

Josh was there to grab the dinghy and hold it still, but it was Denzil who leaned down to help her out.

'Well done,' he congratulated her.

'Who won?' Tory demanded, turning to Josh and flinging her wet hair behind her shoulders.

'Guess you crossed the line together, miss,' he replied with a wide white-toothed grin. 'Lordy, dat was some race! I ain't ever seen a woman sail like dat before.'

Damn, thought Tory, *I wish I'd beaten him*. But there was satisfaction in learning that she hadn't been beaten by him. She'd held her own. If only she hadn't capsized so ignominiously the wrong way.

'I hope you've no more doubts about my ability to sail,' she flashed at Denzil.

'No more doubts,' he conceded. 'After a soaking like that you need a shower and another change of clothes,' he added.

'I'll be all right,' she asserted independently, 'a rub down in the changing room will do. Don't forget my slacks are dry.'

He didn't argue, but when they reached the end of

44

the pontoon he took her arm and guided her in the direction of a path which was shaded by flowering shrubs and palms.

'This isn't the way to the changing room,' she objected. The touch of his hand on her bare skin was possessive and a little disturbing.

'I know it isn't. I'm taking you to my bungalow. You can shower there in peace and privacy.'

'But my slacks ...'

'I'll get them for you.'

She gave in—because she was suddenly curious to see where he lived and not for any other reason, she told herself, refusing to admit that she had no alternative and was being forced to go by the strength of his hand on her arm.

After about five minutes' walk the path ended at a clearing above a small crescent of a beach. Set back from the sand and built on stilts was a wooden bungalow with a verandah running along its front.

They went up a flight of wooden steps to it and entered through a door made of steel mesh into a big living room comfortably furnished with several armchairs and a settee.

'The bathroom is through the archway on the right,' said Denzil. 'You'll find clean towels in a cupboard beside it. I'll go and get your slacks and a dry top for you to wear.'

The bathroom was not as elegant as the one at the Director's house, but the water system was much more efficient, and Tory luxuriated in the feel of hot water washing away the stickiness of salt from her hair and skin.

She had just turned off the shower and was about to pull aside the shower curtain to grope for a towel when the bathroom door, which she had forgotten to lock, opened and froze her to immobility.

'Only me,' said Denzil. 'The dry clothing is on the chair.'

The door closed again. Tory came out of her statuesque stillness, let out her breath and twitched aside the curtain. On the chair were her white slacks and on top of them was a flowered blouse and a pair of bikini panties. Under the chair were her white sandals and her handbag.

She rubbed herself dry, opened the small cupboard above the washbasin and found some men's talc. It had a tangy lemony smell and she used it liberally. The panties fitted perfectly; she slipped her slacks over them and pulled on the blouse. It buttoned down the front and did not fit her as well as the shorts and the panties. It seemed that Denzil's girl-friends weren't as big in the bust as she was, and Tory wished she had been wearing a bra. But even if she had it would have been wet, so she would just have to put up with the fact that the blouse gaped widely between the buttons.

She rubbed her hair dry, combed it back and then made up her face. She picked up the damp towels and hung them over the shower curtain rail. The wet clothing she wrung out in the wash hand basin and leaving the borrowed shorts on the chair rolled her cotton sweater and panties together. She took one quick look round to make sure the place was as tidy as she had found it and stepped out into the passage.

There she paused, curious about what lay behind the two other doors, and moving on tiptoe she went to the first. It was slightly open and as she peered round the edge of it she saw a wide airy room furnished with a double bed and a couple of chests of drawers.

Withdrawing, she went on to the next door. It was also slightly open. Inside was a small narrow room filled with boxes and odds and ends of furniture, obviously used only for storage purposes. It looked very much as if Denzil Hallam's living quarters were designed solely for one person, if she discounted the size of the double bed.

As she made her way back to the living room Tory remembered where she had seen the blouse she was wearing; Carla had one just like it. Colours and pattern were identical to Carla's; tiny multi-coloured flowers scattered over a dark red background.

At once the suspicion that the blouse did belong to Carla and had been left there by the girl on one of her many visits—had possibly been left in this house—sprang into her mind and caused a strange stir of resentment, not against Denzil for persuading the girl to stay, but against Carla who had managed to get into a position which had made it possible for him to persuade her.

Aware that she was thinking irrationally, Tory swung round and stepped purposefully into the living room, determined to disconcert him with a direct question. Shaded by the verandah as well as by blue and white striped awnings over the wide windows which faced west, the room was cooled by a steady sea-breeze which lifted the edges of the long blue and green curtains.

But Denzil wasn't there, so when she heard the sound of whistling she approached the far end of the room and discovered that an archway led into a dining recess that was separated from a kitchen area by a bar-like counter in front of which were some high wooden stools with tops upholstered in bright red vinyl. Beside the counter was another archway leading into the kitchen.

Denzil was in the kitchen and was taking down some tall lemonade glasses from a shelf or cupboard set into the wall above the counter. He set them down on the counter top, looked directly at her and stopped whistling.

'I see the blouse fits where it touches,' he remarked.

'Oh, I might have guessed you'd say something like that,' she retorted, annoyed because she hadn't been able to have the first word after all. 'I don't suppose you have such a thing as a safety pin?'

'No, I never use the things,' he replied, putting his arms on the counter and leaning forward so that he could see her better. 'The gaps between the buttons have a certain tantalising attraction.' His grin widened as she reacted by putting her hand over the largest and middle gap. 'Would you like a glass of iced tea?'

The offer was a surprise. Tea was the last drink she had expected him to offer, and it made her realise suddenly how thirsty she was after the strenuous sail.

'I'd love one,' she said, her hostility in abeyance for a brief moment.

'Then sit down,' he murmured. 'It won't take long to make, it's the instant sort.'

She perched on one of the scarlet-topped stools and placed her wet clothing and handbag on the other. Resting her elbows on the counter top and cupping her chin in her hands, she watched him open a jar and spoon instant tea into the glasses. His movements were quick and efficient and anyone who knew anything about people who sailed about in small boats would know that he had spent a lot of his time on one, she thought, because his kitchen was so spick and span and he put everything he used back in the place from which he had taken it.

'Where's Carla?' she asked as casually as she could, and watched carefully for his reaction.

When it came, it seemed perfectly natural. Denzil turned off the tap from which he had been running cold water into the glasses and glanced at her in surprise.

'How the hell should I know?' he replied. 'I haven't seen her this week.'

CHAPTER THREE

THE answer to her question was so forthright and so ringing with truth that for a moment Tory was the one who was disconcerted as she searched her mind for another way in which to pursue the subject.

Then she remembered the blouse. Taking a point of the collar between her thumb and forefinger, she tugged it to draw his attention to it.

'This is her blouse. I recognise it,' she said.

'Is it?' The answer came back straight away after he had given the blouse another quick survey. 'I wouldn't know.'

He swirled the tawny liquid in the glasses with a swizzle stick, then opened the door of the refrigerator to take out a plastic rack of ice cubes. He put several cubes into each glass, stirred the liquid again and brought the two glasses back to the counter.

'It's evidence that she's been here,' persisted Tory.

'Help yourself,' he said, pushing a glass towards her, 'and tell me why you're playing at being detective.'

'Carla didn't come home last night,' she replied, and curled her hand round the glass, finding the icy coolness a relief to the moist heat of her palm.

Denzil's eyes narrowed and his mouth curved unpleasantly at one corner.

'And what makes you think you'll find her here just because she stayed out all night?' he queried with a smooth silkiness that made her nerves quiver.

She met his hard bright eyes squarely, refusing to be intimidated by his threating expression.

'She's always coming here, and she makes no secret of the fact that she adores you,' she replied coolly.

One of his eyebrows lifted in sardonic amusement, and resting both elbows on the counter he lifted his glass with both hands to take a sip of tea. As he lowered the glass his eyes glinted with mockery.

'This is interesting,' he drawled. 'Please tell me more. For instance, is her father aware of the apparent fascination I have for her?'

'Yes, he is, and it annoys him very much.'

'So he's annoyed and when she's missing he suspects immediately that I'm to blame? Yet he doesn't come looking for her, he sends you instead. What does it feel like to be acting the part of mother when you're not much more than four years older than Carla herself?'

The touch of contempt in his attitude needled her into telling more than she had intended.

'Six years,' she corrected snappishly, 'and I'm not acting the part of mother. Magnus is away, and he asked me to keep an eye on Carla while he's gone. I'd no idea she hadn't come home last night until the housekeeper told me. Naturally I'm very worried, because I wouldn't like Magnus to think I'd let him down.'

'Naturally,' he scoffed. 'You didn't know he had a daughter until he introduced her to you the day you arrived, did you? It was quite a shock to your system to meet her.'

'How do you know?' Tory countered weakly, feeling her cheeks grow warm.

'I had to move slowly that day, if you remember, so I had plenty of time to watch your meeting with him. It struck me as being more than affectionate and I was quite convinced you must be a close relative of his. Instead it turns out you've been hired by the Airounian Department of Parks and Gardens to be his assistant, a nice cosy arrangement engineered by the two of you so that you can work together while you live together,' he jeered.

Tory nearly choked over the tea she was swallowing in reaction to the implication of his remarks, and he was lucky not to have liquid and ice cubes hurled in his face. Cheeks flaming and eyes sparkling, she set the glass down so hard on the counter top that the liquid in it leapt up and splashed over the rim.

'You have a very nasty mind!' she accused furiously.

'It's no worse than yours,' Denzil retorted crisply. 'On the ferryboat you behaved as if you believed I was going to rape you ...'

'I didn't think that,' she gasped.

'Then why did you threaten to scream if I didn't let you pass?'

'I ... I ... you confused me,' she spluttered defensively.

'Really?' he mocked. 'And now today you're implying that I'm the sort of man who would encourage a teenage girl to stay the night with me. Since we've been acquainted for so short a time, I'd say that was rank prejudice on your part.'

Tory took hold of her glass again. Pretending to study the contents of it, she took a stealthy glance at him from beneath her lashes. Temper and pride blazed in his tawny eyes, tautened the skin across his high cheekbones and made his mouth a stern straight line.

'Well, you do encourage Carla,' she muttered, still on the defensive. 'You're always inviting her to come here, she's told me that, but it would be much easier for Magnus to keep her under control if you didn't. He thinks you're too old for her.'

'Yet he doesn't consider himself to be too old for you,' he sniped.

'There's nothing like that between Magnus and me. Oh, I admit I respect and admire him immensely and think that I'm very lucky to have been chosen by him to help him, but that's all we *are* doing together, working, and even if I stay here only a year the experience

51

of working with such a brilliant botanist will be immeasurable.'

'A year? You're going to stay here a whole year?' he exclaimed.

'Yes, and possibly longer,' she said rather smugly. 'The contract is renewable if both parties are agreeable.'

He stared at her not in amusement or annoyance but in amazement before taking another sip of his tea.

'I wonder if you've any idea of what you're letting yourself in for by staying in that house,' he murmured.

'Oh, yes, I have. When he was over in England in the spring Magnus told me all about the job, about the island and the climate, about the people ...'

'But he didn't tell you about Carla,' he interrupted softly. 'And dare I take a guess that he didn't tell you about his wife either?'

'No, he didn't, but as he put it himself, a professor—and that was what he was to me before he came here—rarely discusses his private life with his students,' she said serenely. 'But I know everything now. He's explained.'

'Has he now? And are you quite happy with his explanation?' he queried, and again she had the impression that he was surprised.

'Of course I am, and I'm very pleased that he felt he could confide in me.' She stared at him closely. 'You still think he and I are having an affair, don't you?' she accused.

'My mind was wandering in that direction,' he replied honestly. 'And so are the minds of a few other people on this island.'

'Oh, how stupid!' Tory exclaimed crossly. 'Surely it's obvious that Magnus sees me only as his assistant. Honestly, he does,' she added fiercely when she saw his eyebrows lift in scepticism. 'You don't like him, do you?'

'Shall we say I don't have a very high opinion of a father who's more interested in peering into a microscope than he is in the girl he claims to be his daughter,' he said coldly. 'I suppose it's never occurred to him that Carla comes to the marina because she feels neglected, because she's fed up with being stuck in that big house, because she's bored to desperation with being cooped up with a walking dictionary of botanical terms. She comes not to see me, but in search of people of her own age.'

'Magnus isn't boring,' she defended hotly.

'Not to you, perhaps, because you understand what he's talking about. And that's another thing. Since you came it's been worse for Carla. You now take up whatever spare time he has, so she feels really shut out. I'm sorry for the kid, and that's why I don't turn her away when she comes to the pool, although it's only for the use of yachtsmen and their families who use the marina. And what do I get for my pains? Suspicion of my morals,' he said scathingly.

'Perhaps you've given Magnus reason to suspect them,' she challenged.

'Perhaps I have,' Denzil conceded equably. 'Come to think of it, there have been a couple of reasons since he came to the island.' A faint reminiscent smile curved his mouth. 'One reason was as tall as you are, but she had dark hair. Personally I prefer blondes, even one with grey eyes.'

Irritated by the return of his mockery, Tory would have moved, but he raised a hand and caught her chin between his thumb and fingers. His touch against her face sent a strange sensation shooting along her nerves like the shock from a touch of fire. Determined not to give him any hint of how she was affected, she returned his curious gaze steadily.

'You're right,' he said, looking closely at each of her eyes in turn. 'They're grey without a hint of blue or green, and just now they're the colour of the sea on a stormy day.' He removed his hand, gave her a gentle pat on one cheek before tucking his hand back in the crook of his arm and adding provocatively, 'Don't you ever smile, Victoria?'

She was shaking within, she didn't know why. She knew only that she must get away from this man because he disturbed her in a way no other man ever had. Grabbing her handbag from the other stool, she opened it and took out some money.

'Since you can't tell me where Carla is, I'd better go and look for her in Port Anne,' she said in a tight, controlled voice. 'There are the four dollars for the hire of the dinghy. Thank you for the iced tea. It was very nice.'

She placed the four paper dollars on the counter, intending to slide off the stool and make her way to the door, but he slapped one of his hands down on top of hers so that she couldn't move it away.

'I seem to have said or done something to annoy you,' he drawled.

'Everything you do or say annoys me,' she replied, trying to free her hand and failing. 'I think you're one of the most insufferable men I've ever met and I don't want to waste time talking to you any more.'

'Insufferable!' he exclaimed. 'Oh, come on, that's a bit strong, isn't it? Especially after I let you catch up with me on the last leg of the race so that we could cross the finishing line together and you wouldn't lose your bet.'

'Let me? Let me?' Tory was so angry that she could only splutter. 'You did nothing of the sort,' she spat at him when she had more control. 'I caught up with you because I was able to make my dinghy sail faster than you could make yours. I'm lighter than you are, and ...'

'I agree, you are, and slimmer, although I'm glad to

notice you have curves in all the places a woman should have them, as the blouse conveniently reveals,' he jibed.

'Oh!' She longed to hit him, but one of her hands was still held captive by his and the other was still grasping her handbag. 'Please let go of my hand,' she demanded stiffly.

'So you can slap me?' he queried, with that mocking lift of his eyebrows. 'I'll only let go if you'll stop behaving like the heroine of a Victorian novel who believes her virtue has been outraged. It's a good act, but it doesn't fit in with the rest.'

'Just what do you mean by *the rest*?' she demanded stormily.

'The impression you give of being a cool contemporary type of woman who knows where she's going and how to get there, who can issue a challenge and back it up,' Denzil replied quietly. 'Have you realised we share a common love, Victoria, a love of sailing? It could be a basis for friendship between us, so why don't you tell me where you learned to sail?'

For a moment the change in his tactics held her silent. She sat staring at their hands. His wasn't holding hers so tightly now and the rough warmth of his palm and fingers covered the back of her hand in a subtle caress. Slowly his thumb moved against the tender skin of her wrist where her pulse leapt. The gentle movement sent a tingle up her arm and through her body so that she no longer wanted to pull her hand free. Acknowledging reluctantly that she liked having her hand held by him, she realised that her recent strange and contrary behaviour had been an attempt to protect herself against him. He represented danger. It would be so easy to give in and accept the friendship he offered, but once she had given in she was sure he would take over, and she would lose both her spiritual and physical freedom.

'I learned to sail on a reservoir, near my home in the

north of England,' she said. 'My parents have been members of the sailing club there for years and they've taken my brother George and me sailing with them ever since I can remember. George and I shared the ownership of a racing dinghy until I decided to come to Airouna.' She paused, then added with a touch of defiance, 'I really did catch up on you in the last leg, you know.'

'Because I let you,' he insisted arrogantly. 'Didn't you see me spilling wind out of my sail to slow the boat down?'

'No, I didn't. It's very hard for me to believe anything you say,' she flung back at him.

'That's because you're afraid of me,' he taunted. 'You think that if you believe me you've gone halfway to liking me, and liking me would go against the grain with you, wouldn't it, Victoria?'

She shifted uneasily on the stool and finding he had removed his hand from hers she withdrew her own and clasped it with her other on her handbag, keeping her glance averted because he had come uncomfortably close to guessing the truth about her state of mind.

'I've told you where I learned to sail, now it's your turn to tell me where you learned,' she muttered.

'I picked it up here and there,' he replied vaguely.

'Oh, a very clever answer,' she jibed, lifting her head. 'I suppose it adds to the image you project of the tough enigmatic adventurer. I've heard all about you and how you arrived here after sailing single-handed across the ocean. Why did you do it?'

'For the same reason others do it, for the challenge it presents, that's all,' he said coolly, and she had the impression that he was being wary.

'But why stop at Airouna?'

'Why not?' he countered. 'It's a tropical paradise, the sort most of us dream about living on. I saw a way

56

of making my living, messing about with boats. When Pete de Freitas decided to give up managing it and go and live on Tequila I took over the management of the marina. I don't own the business. It's owned by a development company which has several marinas and charter businesses among the islands. Anything else you'd like to know?'

The edge to his voice warned her that he didn't like being asked personal questions, but she had learned so much in answer to the few she had asked that she was determined to try one more.

'Which part of England do you come from?'

'I'd have thought you'd have guessed by now, lover,' he replied with a grin as he deliberately emphasised the burring accent of his speech.

Lover. It was the casual endearment used by people from the West Country, and now Tory thought about his first name, it should have given her a clue. It was an old British name still used in the ancient stronghold of the Celts, Cornwall.

'Do you come from Fowey, Falmouth, St Austell or St Ives?' she asked.

'You know the Duchy, then?' he countered cautiously.

'Not really. I went to stay with a friend once. Her parents owned a farm near the Helston River. Which town do you come from?'

'Not a town, just a fishing village. You wouldn't know it.'

'In other words you don't want me to know,' she challenged.

'Right, and I'm quite happy with your vague north of England,' he retorted.

'So now I can only assume you left England because something unpleasant happened to you which you'd rather forget,' she murmured, provocative in her turn.

He laughed, a cheerful rollicking sound which showed her exactly what he thought of her suggestion.

'You're really hung up on those Victorian novels, aren't you?' he jeered. 'But weave no romantic fancies about me. Keep them for your admirable professor. I left England because I wanted to leave, because adventure called. I'm here now because I want to be here. Maybe one day adventure will call again and I'll move on.'

'Alone?'

'Now that, Victoria, is a leading question,' he retorted with that devilish twinkle dancing in his eyes. 'It depends on whether I find someone I'd like to come with me.'

They were both leaning on the counter, not opposite to each other but slightly to one side so that the elbow of her bent right arm was touching the elbow of Denzil's right arm. The calmer pace of their conversation, the exchange of information about each other had created a relaxed intimate atmosphere which was emphasised by the shady warmth of the room. Tory discovered that she had forgotten her earlier hostility towards him and was feeling surprisingly at home.

Turning, she found she was so near to him that she could smell his skin, a tantalising tang which was a mixture of salt and sweat. She sensed the warmth of his strong body through the thin stuff of his T-shirt. She could see how thick were the whorls of wiry dark hair against his head, how strong and vigorous the growth was. Above his right eyebrow was a narrow scar; a dark red line showing the marks where stitches had been. Scarcely aware of what she was doing, she touched the scar, tracing the length of it with a forefinger.

'It's healed well,' she murmured.

'It wasn't a very deep gash to start with,' he replied softly, turning his head to look at her so that she felt the warmth of his breath waft across her lips.

At once she had a sudden urgent desire to be kissed by him. Her glance went to his mouth. It was well-shaped. The long upper lip had an amused curve to it while the lower lip thrust forward in a determined sensual line. It was, she decided, the mouth of a man who liked to love dangerously and passionately.

She could have moved away, but she didn't. She stayed quite still, knowing that by not moving she was offering a deliberate invitation to him.

His mouth touched hers gently at first, then more insistently. His fingers caressed her throat and slid round to the back of her neck. Once again the feeling of having been touched by fire flashed through her in a series of shocks which fused into one intense throbbing sensation. Eyes closed, lips parting under the pressure of his, her breasts feeling as if they would burst open the buttons of the too-tight blouse, she found herself wishing quite hard that the counter wasn't between them so that she could press herself against his hard solid body and slide her hands under his T-shirt to caress his warm bare skin.

Instinctively her arms went up to hold him captive, but one of her hands hit the edge of the counter and the sharp rap of wood against flesh and bone jolted her into awareness of what was happening to her, or rather what she was allowing to happen to her.

Reaction set in violently, like a fast ebbing tide. What was she doing, embracing a man she hardly knew in this manner? He wasn't the man she loved. He was a stranger with a doubtful character. So instead of holding him closer she put her hands against him to push him away. He withdrew at once and without looking at him she slid off the stool.

'I must go and find Carla,' she muttered, wiping the back of her hand across her mouth as if by doing so she could wipe out what had happened.

'What's the matter, Victoria? Did you get burned?' Denzil scoffed, and she glanced sideways at him. He was still leaning on the counter, and the hard bright light in his eyes mocked her.

'Not burned, just a little singed,' she retorted as lightly as she could, trying to ignore the trembling in her limbs. 'It sometimes happens when I'm conducting an experiment.'

'So that's what you were doing.' His voice was dry. 'I hope you learned something in the process.'

'Oh, I did,' she replied sweetly, 'but I really must go now. Thanks again for the sail and the tea. Goodbye.'

She was across the room and in the long living room before he had replied. Almost running, she went through the screen door and blundered down the wooden steps and along the shady pathway. When she emerged from the shade into the glare of sunlight on pale gravel she groped automatically for her sunglasses, and discovered that she was still quivering with reaction.

She shoved the glasses into place and pretended that it was the glare which had caused tears to rush suddenly into her eyes, and she didn't turn when she heard Denzil's voice behind her calling her name and asking her to wait, but went on towards the car park and the comparative safety of the cream car.

The edges of the car key were sharp against the moist softness of her palm as she inserted it into the lock of the door. She turned the key, heard the lock slide back and pulled the key out, but before she could put her hand on the handle to open the door another hand was there, a big hand which was tanned the colour of teak, a hand she recognised only too well.

She stood and waited, not looking round.

'You forgot something,' he said quietly, and surprise

forced her to look round and up. Beneath the slanted peak of his yachting cap his eyes shone with the same hard brilliance as he looked down at her. He was holding out his other hand, and in it was a roll of money. When she didn't move to take it from him he leaned forward and stuffed it in the breast pocket of the too-tight blouse. As his knuckles brushed against her breast another flash-fire flame seemed to streak through her.

'Your winnings,' he added. 'You bet I'd find you as good a sailor as I am. I took you on for the hire of the dinghy. You won.'

Tory was glad of the protective screen of the sunglasses, because once again those stupid tears were gathering in her eyes. His face looked rather blurred, but she saw his brows slanting together in a frown as she hesitated, and knew she must make an effort to appear cool and in control of herself if she didn't want him asking her what was wrong again. So she smiled, rather tremulously,

'Thank you,' she said.

'I knew I'd like it when you smiled,' he murmured gently. ' 'Bye, Victoria.'

He waited until she had started the car and had driven it to the entrance. As she stopped there to look out for any passing traffic she glanced in the rear-view mirror and saw him walking away towards the pontoons.

Tory didn't drive into Port Anne to look for Carla as had been her intention when she left the marina, because she was too disturbed by what had happened between herself and Denzil, so she turned left and took the winding road over the hill to the valley, back to the Director's house, back to the botanical laboratory and the experiments over which she had more control.

Never again would she go to the marina to see Denzil! Never again would she risk close contact with him. Considering how that close embrace had brought to life her female instincts, turning her on in a way that had never happened to her before when she had been kissed by a man, it would be safer for her to avoid him. No, never again dared she risk playing with the fire of physical passion.

What irritated her most, she found, was that she had more or less asked him to kiss her. She had behaved with most unusual abandon, first by touching the scar on his face and then by responding to his kiss, and there was no doubt in her mind what would have happened if the counter had not been between them. She would not now be driving back to the Botanical Gardens!

What had made her invite him to kiss her? As she drove almost blindly round the swinging curves of the road, safe in the knowledge that no traffic would be coming the other way, Tory searched her mind frantically for a reason and came up with one. Propinquity, that had been the reason. Being so close to him, sensing the comfort his warmth and strength offered, she had wanted to make contact. But why? Because she was lonely?

She lonely? Here on this lovely island, where she was working with the man she admired most and with whom she wanted to be most of all? The whole idea was ludicrous and she did actually laugh as she drove between the stone gateposts that marked the entrance to the Gardens.

As always, the sight of graceful white poinsettia trees drooping gracefully above the shimmering blue pool soothed her. A group of brazenly pink flamingoes ruffled their plumage as she drove past and high against the blue sky the blossoms of the pink poui tree echoed the colour of their feathers. The big white house was dreaming in the yellow glow of the late afternoon sun and it was with a sense of having reached a peaceful haven after being tossed about on the stormy sea of passion that Tory went up the steps and entered the cool hallway.

Mrs Dunnet was there, crossing the shining wooden floor on her way from the stairs to the kitchen. She paused when she heard Tory enter and her eyes brightened.

'Dat girl is back home,' she said. 'She stayed de night with Mrs Campos, so I guess dat's okay?'

'Who is Mrs Campos?' asked Tory, making her way to the stairs.

'She's an old school friend of Mrs Jarrold's, and she and her husband have a place up on the coast, north of Port Anne.'

Evidently Mrs Dunnet felt she had said enough because she gave one of her bird-like nods and scurried away into the kitchen.

Tory ran up the stairs to her room. There she changed into a green and white striped cotton dress and brushed her hair which was now completely dry. Then, picking up Carla's blouse, she went along to the girl's room. Her knock was answered by a request to enter and she went in to find Carla sprawled on the bed listening to rock music on her transistor radio. When she saw Tory and the blouse, she flicked off the radio and sat up with a bounce.

'That's my blouse,' she said in her abrupt manner. 'Where did you get it?'

'At the marina. You left it there.'

'What did you go there for?' Carla demanded, scowling suddenly.

'To look for you. You might have let me know that you were going to stay out all night. It would have saved me a lot of bother,' replied Tory curtly. She was becoming very tired of Carla's lack of manners.

63

'I've told you,' said Carla with a long sigh of weariness as if she were also tired of dealing with someone as dense as Tory appeared to be, 'that you have no authority over me. I didn't have to tell you that I wouldn't be home.'

'But you could have told Mrs Dunnet,' retorted Tory. 'She prepared meals for you, and I would have liked to have known because I promised your father I'd keep an eye on you.'

'And of course you have to keep in his good books, don't you?' jeered Carla. 'It would be too bad if his new protégée slipped from grace because she failed to keep an eye on me.' Her slanting black glance raked Tory. 'You might as well give up trying to win me over to your side, you know, because it won't work. I don't like you, I'll never like you and I don't want you here. You could never be a substitute for my mother, which is the position you're aiming for, so will you please get out of my room and leave me in peace?'

Anger scorched through Tory and she was very tempted to let fly with a few home truths. Just in time she saw the glint of malice in Carla's eyes and realised that was what the girl wanted her to do; get involved in a slanging match which would be reported to Magnus and add to the anxiety he already felt about Carla.

So, tightening her lips on the hot words which she longed to fling at the girl, Tory turned and left the room, thinking how glad she would be when Magnus returned the next day.

And she was glad, although the feeling was not as intense as she had expected it to be. It seemed to have lost some of its joyousness, because the sight of his tall slight figure, boyish features and longish rust-coloured hair did not have the same impact as usual.

That was because he had not been away for very long and because she was more used to seeing him, she decided, refusing to believe that possibly he was no longer attractive to her.

He had been back only a day and she was with him in his study, working on the book, when the door crashed open and Carla came storming in, her hair bouncing and crackling as if each strand of it carried a live electrical current, and her dark eyes flashed sparks. Ignoring, as usual, her father's mild and ineffectual remarks that she should knock before she entered when he was working, she turned on Tory.

'What did you say about me to Denzil when you were at the marina?' she demanded.

'Very little,' retorted Tory coolly. 'Why do you ask?'

'He says I'm not to go swimming any more at the pool. He says I'm not to hang around there.'

'So what's wrong with that?' said Tory, still calm, wondering why Denzil had taken action. 'The pool is for the use of people who keep their yachts at the marina or for people chartering boats. It isn't open to the public.'

'Tory's quite right,' Magnus said. 'Now will you please go away, Carla? We're very busy.'

'I don't care if you are,' cried Carla, her eyes bright now with the sparkle of tears. 'It's all your fault,' she almost shouted at Tory, 'if you hadn't gone there and said something to Denzil about me he wouldn't have done anything about it. Now I've nowhere to go, nothing to do. Oh, I wish Mummy were here.'

She whirled and ran suddenly from the room. The door crashed closed behind her, and for a few moments there was silence in the room. Then Magnus pushed his glasses up on to his head, leaned back in his chair and rubbed his eyes with the tips of his fingers.

'I'd no idea you'd been to see Hallam,' he said with a touch of weariness. 'You didn't tell me.'

'I didn't think it was necessary to tell you,' she de-

fended. She had decided not to mention the fact that
Carla had stayed out for the night while he had been
away, so as not to worry him. 'She was missing one day,
so I went to look for her. I tried the marina first.'

'Did you find her there?'

'No, Mr Hallam said he hadn't seen her all week.
He wanted to know why I'd gone there to search and I
told him how you felt about Carla visiting the place.'

'That was very brave of you, Tory,' Magnus said,
removing his fingers from his eyes and smiling at her.
'I hope he wasn't rude to you?'

'Well, he wasn't very pleased, and he told me that
he regards Carla only as a teenager who's looking for
companionship of her own age, and that she'd found
it at the marina, so he'd turned a blind eye and allowed
her to go on using the pool.'

'Thus encouraging her to defy me,' he put in.

'But he didn't deliberately encourage her, he told
me that, and the fact that he's told her not to go again
shows that he appreciates how you feel about her going
there, doesn't it?'

'Yes, I suppose it does.' His mouth tilted wryly.
'Doesn't it seem odd to you that Hallam has more
control over my daughter than I have myself? That
he's been able to achieve at one meeting with her what
I couldn't achieve during the past few months?'

'He has a way of speaking ...' Tory began by way of
explanation.

'I know. He's the masterful type and I'm not,' he
said with a touch of bitterness. 'Well, your effort to
help seems to have produced some rather violent results, judging by her behaviour just now. I expect she's
going to treat us to a few days of the sulks, and living
in this place will become unbearable. Did you ever
find out where she actually did go?'

'Yes, to a Mrs Campos. Mrs Dunnet seemed to know

of her and was quite satisfied.'

'Oh, so Lise is back, is she? I must have a word with her. She and my wife went to school together. She, like Rita, is a member of one of the old Portuguese families who came to Airouna years ago to help grow sugar and found trading centres. She has a couple of teenage children—in fact her daughter must be about the same age as Carla, but not, I suspect, such a problem. Whatever am I going to do with her?'

It was an appeal for more help than Tory was able to give, because she knew now that Carla and she would never hit it off. For a moment she stared at him as he sat, head in hands, elbows on his desk, obviously worrying quite ineffectually about the girl and not having the slightest idea of how to deal with her.

'Could I make a suggestion?' she asked tentatively.

'Of course, my dear.'

'Is it possible for Carla to go and stay with Mrs Campos for a few days? A change of scene and company might help her to recover from the disappointment of not being able to go to the marina any more.'

'Tory, you're a marvel,' Magnus smiled his relief. 'I don't know why I didn't think of it myself. I'll get in touch with Lise straight away ... or at least as soon as we've finished those notes.'

And so it was arranged, and Carla went off to stay with Lise Campos and her daughter for a week. Peace and quiet descended once more on the Director's house. Days slipped by, always sunny, with the occasional rain shower brought by the steady trade wind that kept the temperature from soaring too high.

Work at the Gardens went on in its usual tranquil rhythm. Flowers bloomed in profusion, producing psychedelic flashes of colour, and every day Tory was fascinated by the way the hibiscus mutabilis changed colour from white in the morning to delicate rose pink at noon through deeper and deeper pink all afternoon, to end as dull red before it closed its petals in the evening.

She gave her first talk on gardening to a group of enthusiastic islanders in a church hall in Port Anne. Nervous at first, she warmed to her theme when she found that her audience listened quietly and appreciatively. Some of the listeners came forward afterwards to invite her to see their gardens so that she could give them on-the-spot advice about which plants they should grow. Tory accepted the invitations happily, knowing that they meant she had been accepted by the friendly people.

Yes, work was going well and her relationship with Magnus too seemed to be making progress, although so far he had not shown by any word or action that he regarded her with any more fondness than he might have for an old and trusted friend.

But it would take time for him to realise she could be more than that, she told herself on the Friday of that week, as she dressed in her delphinium blue gown for the first real social occasion since she had arrived in Airouna; a reception held in Government House for all the people in government employment and which Magnus had insisted she should attend in his company.

The reception was held in a large white room, glittering with mirrors and chandeliers, which was on the ground floor of the beautiful eighteenth-century building situated on a hill overlooking Port Anne. Drinks and savoury titbits were served, and gradually as the room became more and more crowded the noise level rose until it was impossible to speak to anyone without shouting at them or leaning very close to them.

The temperature rose too, even though the long jalousied windows were open to the sea breeze. Faces both white and black began to shine. Many a masculine brow was mopped with a handkerchief, and many a woman had cause to glance surreptitiously into one of the mirrors, to gasp in dismay at a wilting hairdo or melting mascara.

Finding herself alone and cut off from Magnus, who was apparently trapped against a wall by the portly middle-aged man with steel-grey hair and a swarthy aquiline face who was Harold Ribiera, Chairman of the Department of Parks and Gardens, Tory decided to slip out through a nearby window on to a terrace to cool off.

It took time to sidle through the chattering laughing groups, but she had almost reached the window when one of her hands was grasped and held tightly. One tug and she was jerked round to face Denzil Hallam's wickedly glinting eyes.

'If I'd known you were going to be here I wouldn't have made a date to have dinner with someone else,' he said. 'Why haven't you been to sail a dinghy again?'

A smoothly fitting cream safari jacket made from lightweight suiting and a green shirt which matched the flecks in his eyes tamed the toughness slightly, but he still looked vaguely piratical and for a moment she felt a pang of disappointment because he had a date with someone else.

'I ... I've been busy,' she muttered, trying to free her hand from his.

'Conducting experiments with your dear professor?' he taunted daringly. 'The two of you have certainly turned a few heads and wagged a few tongues here tonight!'

'What do you mean? Whose heads and tongues?' she demanded.

'Those that belong to the people who matter, the wives of the politicians and civil servants, the social élite of Airouna.'

'I don't see why I should draw their attention more than anyone else,' she countered.

'Then obviously you're one of the few women here tonight who hasn't looked in a mirror lately,' Denzil murmured. His hard bright glance flicked over her. 'Silver-gilt hair, golden peach-bloom tan and a simple blue dress that draws attention to your far from insignificant charms. It's not quite as revealing as Carla's blouse, perhaps, but it flatters you, and ... yes ... I do believe it makes your eyes seem just slightly more blue than grey.'

'I wish you'd let go of my hand,' she whispered, frantically trying to free it from his grasp and at the same time looking round to see if anyone nearby had noticed how closely he was standing to her.

'Why is it you don't like having your hand held in mine?' he mocked, leaning closer to her so that she could smell the scents of the soap and the talc he used and the sweet-sharp tang of the rum he had drunk. 'Does it turn you on when least expected?' he added outrageously.

'You are ...' she began furiously.

'Insufferable, I know,' he agreed with a grin. 'But seriously, do you think it was wise for you to come to an affair like this with your professor, to walk into this nest of gossips with your arm through his?'

'I was invited to come with him,' she retorted. 'I wish I knew what you're talking about.'

From beneath her lowered lashes she saw his eyes narrow, his thick dark lashes almost covering the clear bright gleam as he considered her.

'That air of innocent bewilderment is amazing,' he scoffed. 'I wonder how you do it? I could almost believe that you really don't know, only last time we met you told me that you did.' He leaned closer and she felt her cheek tingle as his hair brushed against it. 'Supposing his wife comes back,' he whispered. 'What are you going to do?'

She shivered in that hot close room and clung to his hand for support. Then common sense asserted itself.

'I think that sort of joke is in very bad taste,' she snapped, leaning back, away from him. 'She can't come back because she isn't alive.'

'Did he tell you that?' he demanded sharply.

'Not in so many words, but when I asked him about her he couldn't talk, so I just assumed that she'd died.'

'What about Carla? Doesn't she mention her mother?'

'No ... well, only once, and that was to wish her mother was here.' Tory became aware that he was looking at her in a very strange way, almost as if he pitied her. 'Denzil, if you know something that I don't know but should know, please tell me,' she asked in an urgent whisper.

His mouth quirked mockingly and he released her hand.

'I know lots of things you don't know, but I'm not at all sure I should tell you about them. Many of them aren't suitable for the ears of an innocent abroad, as you pretend to be,' he taunted lazily, letting his glance rove round the room.

'You know something about Rita Jarrold,' she accused.

'Do I?' His glance came back to her to mock her.

'Please tell me,' she pleaded.

He raised his hand, pushed back the cuff of his sleeve and studied his watch.

'It's time I left,' he murmured. 'Nice seeing you again, Victoria, even if it was for such a short time. Doing anything over the week-end?'

'I shall probably do some shopping, a little swimming and sunbathing and some reading,' she replied coolly.

'Sounds exciting,' he jibed. 'I could use a deckhand if you're interested in having a cruise down to Tequila and back. I promised some people who are going to spend a week there that I'd take them myself.'

'On your own boat? You still have it, then?' she asked, her interest suddenly roused.

'Yes, she's part of the charter fleet. If you decide to come, be at the marina by eight o'clock in the morning. If you don't turn up on time I won't wait, but will assume you have other things to do—like conducting experiments with the dear professor.'

CHAPTER FOUR

THE path from the Botanical Gardens over the hill to the part of the road that ran past the entrance to the marina—that short cut once mentioned by Magnus—was well-worn; trodden many times during the past few months, Tory suspected, by Carla. It climbed steeply through the rain-forest under primeval trees bearded with moss and festooned by airplants and vines whose twining branches were as thick as a man's leg. Huge ferns and wide spade-like leaves created a green gloom that was broken only occasionally by thin shafts of yellow sunlight. And everywhere the forest was alive with the morning shouts and whistles of many birds.

As she stepped over fallen branches and ducked under trailing vines, Tory wished she had time to examine some of the flowers that glowed and twinkled, like stars of crimson, yellow and white in a dark green sky, but she was in a hurry to reach the marina before eight o'clock because she didn't want Denzil to leave for Tequila without her.

She wasn't sure why she had decided she would accept his casual invitation to crew for him; she only knew that she had decided it when she had gone to bed the previous night.

On the way home from the reception Magnus had been silent and preoccupied and she had not disturbed him with chatter, but had sat in the semi-darkness of the car thinking of Denzil and how tormenting he could be, how cruel, as if he were determined to shake her trust in Magnus. His suggestion that Rita Jarrold might come back had been macabre and had stirred up remembrances of novels such as *Wuthering Heights* and *Jane Eyre*, which she had read at school. The last-named story haunted her in particular as she had sat at dinner with Magnus in the Director's house, and she had even found herself wondering in which room Rita Jarrold was locked away because she was mad.

And then she had looked across the flickering flames of candles and had almost laughed aloud. No one looking at Magnus could possibly confuse him with Mr Rochester, the passionate, domineering hero of *Jane Eyre*.

'I have to fly to St Thomas tomorrow morning,' he had said, coming out of his abstraction. 'Some family business to attend to. I might not be able to get back until Monday, so you're free for the entire weekend, my dear. What will you do?'

'I might go sailing,' she said.

'Oh. I didn't know you were interested in the activity. You never told me,' he remarked, and she had been unable to stop smiling at his obvious pique because he didn't know everything about her.

'I could say that a student rarely has the opportunity to discuss her spare-time pursuits with her professor.' She hadn't been able to resist mocking him a little and had been surprised when he looked hurt.

'But you and I are beyond that stage now, surely. We're friends and professional colleagues,' he said. 'We *are* friends, aren't we, Tory?' His blue glance above the flame-topped tapers was anxiously appealing, and she had capitulated at once.

'Yes, of course. You should know by now that I'd do anything for you, Magnus,' she said breathlessly, going all the way, committing herself impulsively. For a moment their glances had met above the yellow flames and he had reached forward to place his hand over hers where it rested on the table.

'Thank you,' he said simply, 'I appreciate very much

74

what you've just said. You're a very sweet person, Tory, and your dedication to our work, your devotion to me personally, have helped enormously during the past few weeks.' His eyebrows twitched together and his mouth thinned. 'Life hasn't been too easy for me during the past year. There have been problems, difficulties ...' His voice died away and once again she had sensed that he could not talk about his unhappiness.

'I understand,' she said quickly, and he flicked a glance at her, a curious puzzled glance.

'I hope you do, my dear, I hope you do,' he murmured, withdrawing his hand, and they both left the table to walk together into the hall. At the foot of the stairs they halted as if by mutual agreement. He raised a hand and had touched her hair, lifting a stray strand that had slipped forward across her brow and laying it back in place.

'If you go sailing tomorrow tell Mrs Dunnet, please,' he said. 'Carla should be returning on Sunday evening, so I'm afraid our quiet time will be at an end. Now if you'll excuse me, I have to make preparations for my journey tomorrow, so I'll say goodnight.'

'Goodnight, Magnus,' Tory whispered, hoping he would read the message in her eyes correctly, and it seemed as if he had, for he leaned forward and kissed her on the lips and with another muttered 'goodnight', turned and walked away quickly to the study.

Tory should have gone up the stairs with springing steps and a heart that sang, but she hadn't. She had trudged up with her head bowed, conscious of a flat feeling of anticlimax because Magnus had kissed her and nothing had happened.

The shimmer of sunlight on blue water alerted her to the fact that she had come through the green tunnel of tropical foliage and that the path was descending towards the road and she came out of the flashback of her thoughts into the present again and the need to hurry because she guessed that Denzil Hallam would wait for no woman or man.

Soon she was entering the marina, and realised that she had no idea where Denzil's boat was berthed, or even what it was called. A few people were moving about the pontoons preparing to go sailing, and as she approached the steps that led up to the door of the office building the door opened and Denzil came out. He saw her at once, ran down the steps, lifted his yachting cap briefly from his head and set it back at an angle.

'What brought you?' he queried tauntingly, standing before her his hands on his hips while his hard glance surveyed her from head to foot. 'Curiosity about Rita Jarrold or a longing to be near me?'

'Neither,' she said between her teeth. 'I came because I want to go sailing. And stop looking at me like that, as if I'm an article that you're considering buying. I'm not for sale.'

'Sharp in the morning, aren't you?' he countered. 'What's wrong? Didn't the professor come up to scratch last night?'

'Oh, you ... I'm sorry I came!' she retorted wildly, and turned to leave, feeling those tears which Denzil seemed so adept at rousing start into her eyes. Immediately he caught her by the arm.

'Okay, I'm sorry, that last remark was out of line. My only excuse is that I got out of bed the wrong side myself this morning after a bad night,' he murmured. 'And I was looking you over to make sure you were properly dressed. I hope you've brought something thin with long sleeves to cover your arms.'

'No, I haven't,' she admitted.

'I'm afraid your arms might get burnt, your skin is so fair. Any objections to wearing a man's cotton pyjama jacket if I bring one for you?' he asked. 'You'll find it very effective without being too hot and cumber-some.'

The change in his attitude from carelessness to caring had the effect of mesmerising her, so that she nodded her agreement almost without realising it.

'Good, then go to the boat ... you'll find it berthed at the end of number four pontoon. You can't miss it because it has canvas dodgers protecting the cockpit, with the name on them—*Ariel*. The passengers are already aboard making themselves at home. You can start taking the cover off the mainsail.'

He went off in the direction of the path to his bungalow and Tory found the pontoon and made her way along it. The boat was a sturdy-looking vessel built of wood. Its mast was short and well-rigged for ocean sailing. Tory stepped aboard and introduced herself to the two women and two men who were sitting round the cockpit. They were in all their middle twenties and obviously excited about the forthcoming sail.

Stepping past them, Tory made her way through the hatchway, down a narrow ladder into the main cabin of the boat to stow the canvas holdall in which she had brought a change of clothing, some nightwear and a bikini. At once she was impressed by the size and airi-ness of the accommodation. There were two wide settee berths with a folding table between them, and a galley with an oven and sink. Under the berths and beside them were lockers with sliding doors, and opposite the galley was a chart table with navigational aids set above it on shelves, including a ship-to-shore radio.

The woodwork was well varnished and a peep through a door near the mast showed her that there was a lavatory and washing facilities up forward. There was, in fact, everything a long-distance sailor would require, she thought, taking a minute longer to look around, and everything was of the best quality. Denzil might have been ragged, half-starved and have had no money to speak of when he had arrived in Airouna, but his boat had cost money to build and equip.

A shout from the hatchway turned her round just in time to see a plain green pyjama jacket fall through the opening to the floor of the cabin. Quickly she slipped out of her polyester sleeveless top and pulled on the jacket. It was very wide and a little long in the sleeves, but she realised that its large size and the thinness of the cotton would be both protective and airy.

Back on deck she was soon busy obeying Denzil's crisp orders. Apparently the two men passengers were keen-to help and it wasn't long before the boat had cleared the pontoon and the sails were being hoisted as it forged across the bay in the direction of the open sea.

The course to Tequila was due south-east from Airouna and since the trade wind blew from the northeast it was an easy reaching sail. Mainsail and foresail full and curved, the boat bounded over waves crested with silvery foam. Standing on the foredeck, her legs braced against the movement of the deck beneath her feet, feeling the wind in her hair and the sting of spray on her skin, Tory experienced a freedom of spirit she had never known before. Ahead the sun laid a path of gold upon the blue sea, a path which seemed to beckon temptingly, inviting the sailor to follow it for ever.

Within two and a half hours a small blue hump rose up out of the sea, and within another hour the island had taken on shape and colour. It was crowned by a tangle of green trees and edged by pale sand and sparkling white surf, and it looked deserted. As the boat approached closer the land seemed to shift. An opening appeared at the end of what appeared to be a ridge of sand. The boat altered course and the sails were trimmed accordingly as it made straight for the opening, and soon they were entering a lagoon of placid turquoise water shading to clear limpid green where it touched a curving beach overhung by graceful palm trees.

It was not until the boat was anchored that Tory noticed the small stone jetty jutting out from the shore. A launch was detaching itself from the side of the jetty. Its outboard engine roared into life and soon it was alongside the yacht. The passengers stepped over the side into the launch, their luggage was handed down to them, and with a few cheery waves and shouted goodbyes they were gone.

Looking up from furling the mainsail round the boom and tying it with a strip of terylene, Tory saw that beyond the jetty, half hidden by the drooping fronds of the palms, was a building of grey stone which extended parallel to the beach. It seemed to consist of a solid wall on which a wooden structure with wide windows had been built.

'I'd no idea there was a building,' she exclaimed to Denzil as he came to help her finish tying up the sail. 'It isn't noticeable from the water.'

'That's the idea,' he replied. 'That building is the dining pavilion of the hotel which is Pete de Freitas's pride and joy. The bedrooms are in single cottages, twenty of them scattered about the island, built in traditional West Indian style, solid and comfortable yet unobtrusive. When everything is ship-shape we'll go ashore to see Pete. He has a cottage on that point of land over there. Did you enjoy the sail?'

'Yes, it was lovely. I like your boat too, not too small and not too big—just right for one person, I suppose.'

'But actually fitted out for two, or hadn't you noticed?' he remarked dryly. 'You're a good crew, Victoria. Quick and neat, and you don't answer back.'

'I wouldn't be too sure about the not answering back, if I were you,' she retorted. 'I was on my best behaviour in front of your passengers, so don't get too rough with your orders, skipper. If you swear at me I'll swear right back!'

'Tut, tut,' he scoffed, leaning his arms on the boom and grinning at her. 'What would your professor say?'

The sail over the blue sea under the hot sun seemed to have liberated her. Mischief sprang up, and reaching over she snatched his cap from his head and sent it flying through the air like a frisbee to land with a tiny splash on the water.

'You little devil,' he murmured threateningly, and ducked under the boom to grab her and lift her up in his arms. 'In you go to rescue it before it sinks!'

He stepped down from the cabin roof on to the side-deck and lifted her high above the wire lifelines which, strung between steel stanchions, ran round the boat about two feet higher than the deck. Kicking her legs and pummelling at his shoulders, Tory tried to free herself when she realised he had every intention of dropping her into the water.

'No, Denzil, please! Don't drop me in. I promise I'll get it for you, only let me dive. I couldn't bear to be dropped. There might be sharks.'

'Not a chance,' he retorted, and raised her up again.

'No ... no ...!' Tory's voice rose to a screech which was cut off suddenly as instead of dropping her into the water he closed her mouth with his own in a hard kiss. Her legs were lowered so she could stand and he put his freed arm around her to hold closely.

Effectively silenced, Tory found she no longer wanted to struggle. Through the thinness of the pyjama jacket she felt the hardness of his chest bruising the softness of her breasts, sending sharp stabbing sensations through her so that she went dizzy with a new desire to press closer to him, to relax the control of her mind over her body, to float on the sea of passion his touch aroused.

'Mister 'Allam, is dis your 'at?'

The voice was boyish and had a warm throaty chuckle. Through the haze of sensuousness which was enveloping her, making her reckless about what happened next, Tory felt Denzil stiffen. He took his mouth from hers and his hand on the back of her neck pushed her face into his warm shoulder as he spoke to someone behind her.

'It is, Billy. Throw it into the cockpit, will you? I'll see you later with a reward for rescuing it. Right now, I'm busy.'

'You sure is, Mister 'Allam, I can see dat. You sure is.'

The chuckling voice was followed by the creak of oars in rowlocks and the splashing sound of oarblades slicing through water.

'You coming ashore?' Billy asked from a litle further away.

'Later. I'll give you a shout when I want you to come for us,' replied Denzil.

'Okay, boss.'

The creaking and splashing sounds drifted away. Tory moved, pushing her head back against his hand, and looked up to encounter narrowed black-lashed gleaming eyes.

'Well, Victoria, what now? Shall we go below to continue what you've started in more privacy and comfort?' he asked.

'I haven't started anything. It was you with your taunts about Magnus,' she protested, trying to free herself only to find that she was caught in a circle by his arms.

'You didn't have to throw my hat in the water,' he murmured.

'And you didn't have to kiss me,' she retorted.

'What other way is there to stop a woman from howling like a banshee?' he mocked. 'You didn't have to kiss me back. I'm only human, after all, a very susceptible male, and when a desirable woman like you kisses me as you've just done I see it as an open invitation to make love to her.'

His voice softened and his hands moved to her waist. She felt the roughness of them against her smooth skin under the loose pyjama jacket, sliding upwards as he bent his head, his glance on her mouth, his lips parting slightly.

'It wasn't an invitation,' she mumbled desperately, leaning back, away from him, her limbs weak and full of a longing to lie down. 'I don't want you to make love to me because I don't love you and you don't love me, so will you please take your hands off me?'

'Whom do you love, then? The professor?' he scoffed, his hands back at her waist, holding her lightly as he slanted a glance down at her. 'Poor little Victoria, bursting with love for a man who's frozen from the neck down ...'

'He isn't!'

'Has he ever kissed you?'

'Yes ... but ...' She stopped, realising she had just been about to give herself away. 'He's shy, diffident.'

'So nothing happened,' he jeered. 'No wonder you react the way you do when you're really kissed. You're just longing to give and he doesn't want you.'

'Because something doesn't happen the first time you kiss a person it doesn't prove anything, any more than if something does happen,' she countered furiously. 'Love isn't all physical.'

'But a large percentage of it is, and should be,' Denzil retorted. 'For a scientist you're not very good at deducing from the results of your experiments, are you? And how anyone like you can waste your time on a man who doesn't care for you, I can't understand. You're a fool, Victoria, and heading for a fall.'

'Well, it's my business, isn't it?' she retorted shakily. 'And I can't think why you concern yourself with it.'

'No, I don't suppose you can,' he said with a sigh, removing his hands at last from her waist and turning away. 'Get your hat and sunglasses and your swimming things if you've brought them. I'll call Billy back.'

Down in the cabin Tory took off the pyjama jacket and put on her sleeveless striped top. She rolled her bikini in a towel, trying to ignore the fact that her fingers were shaking as a result of the tumult of her feelings. Once again a confrontation with Denzil had led to an explosion of passion which had been expressed by physical contact, and she was disturbed by the fact that beneath the surface of all their meetings a mutual sexual attraction lay like a land-mine hidden beneath pleasant countryside, awaiting only the lightest touch to erupt and wreak devastation.

It must be the heat, she decided in an attempt to assert her control over herself. Hadn't she read somewhere that the tropical sun at noon had a relaxing effect on the inhibitions, causing men and women to discard the usual controls and express their most violent feelings in word and deed?

No, that explanation wouldn't do either, because it presumed that she and Denzil felt violently and passionately about each other, and she didn't want to admit that he aroused in her a fiery turbulence which she was afraid might be the hate that is so akin to love.

Hair smooth beneath her hat, sunglasses in place to hide any betraying expression there might be in her eyes, her white shorts crisp and neat, showing off the tan of her long legs, her striped top taut and smooth against breasts and waist, she went on deck looking cool and self-assured.

As she stepped over the side of the yacht into the

small rowing dinghy and took her place on the thwart in the bow, she heard Denzil introducing her to the teenage boy who was sitting on the middle thwart holding the oars.

'This is Victoria, Billy,' he drawled casually as he stepped down into the stern of the dinghy.

The boy gave her a brief shy glance over his shoulder and nodded. Turning back to face Denzil, who was now sitting, he said,

'She your wife?'

'Not yet.'

'Going to be?'

'Maybe.'

Over the boy's shaven bullet head Victoria glared at Denzil, but he wasn't looking at her, and belatedly she remembered the sunglasses so the whole effect was lost, which infuriated her more. She stared at Bill's back and thought how thin he was; the bones showed white through his bare chocolate-brown skin as he pulled on the oars, moving forwards and backwards with graceful rhythm to send the wooden boat skimming across the smooth shimmering water towards the long snout of green-topped, white-edged land which formed the northern shore of the lagoon.

When the dinghy nudged against a small stone jetty, a large man in a flower-patterned shirt and white cotton pants who had been waiting for their arrival reached down to help Tory ashore.

'Hello there,' he boomed. 'That was a fine bit of entertainment you and Denzil put on for the locals. Better than going to the movies, Mandy says. We were watching you through the binoculars. I'm Pete de Freitas.'

'Her name is Victoria,' said Denzil coolly as he came to stand beside them. 'And you have to watch what you say to her, because she has a tendency to react like the heroine of a Victorian novel. She works for Magnus Jarrold at the Gardens. Is Mandy up at the house?'

'Yes, getting your favourite drink ready.'

'Good, I want a word with her.'

Denzil strode away up the jetty while Tory and Pete moved along at a more leisurely pace.

'Welcome to Tequila, Victoria,' said Pete, whose mixed island heritage was revealed in his aquiline features, swarthy skin and pale eyes which blazed like blue flames in the darkness of his face.

'Thank you, but I prefer to be called Tory,' she replied. 'Denzil uses my full name to torment me.'

'Is that so?' said the large man with a chuckle. 'Now I wonder why he would want to torment someone as pretty as you are? Has he told you anything about this island and how long it's taken me to develop it as a holiday resort?'

'No. I haven't come into contact with him very often, and I've only come today because he said he needed someone to crew for him on the boat.'

His crackle of laughter was scornful.

'And you fell for that? He doesn't need anyone to crew for him. He can handle that boat alone. He asked you to come for some other reason, and I wouldn't mind guessing that it was because he wanted female company, the prettier the better, make no mistake about that. And Mandy, she's my wife, is going to be glad he's brought you. There's nothing she likes more than a visit from a youngster like you. She'll pester you to death with questions about England, your family, your work—especially your work when she hears you're with Doc Jarrold.'

'Is she from Airouna too?' asked Tory. They were walking over the soft sand, now, floundering a little as their feet slipped on its dryness.

'Yes, she is, a mixture like the rest of us with a drop

85

of real Carib blood mixed in with the African, English and Portuguese blood. We were married three years ago when she came back from the States after nursing there for nearly twenty years.' Pete's laugh shook his massive body. 'Neither of us ever expected to find someone we'd like to marry so late, but as soon as we met— snap, that was it.'

Mandy was tall and brown-skinned. She moved about with a slow rhythmic walk and hummed a tune as she set long glasses full of fruit punch on a round table set between four loungers on the verandah of the thatched hut she and Pete called home.

She was wearing a red-flowered dress which flattered her full-breasted, majestic figure, and had an air of sophistication which she had probably acquired during her years in a big American city. She was about ten years younger than Pete, forty to his fifty, Tory guessed, and she talked in a slow drawl, her speech scattered with American idioms and dry humorous remarks.

As Pete had predicted, Mandy was full of questions and listened to Tory's answers with an interest that flattered, but it wasn't until they were having lunch in the big airy room behind the verandah, helping themselves from wooden bowls of marinated seafood, breadfruit soufflé and sliced peppers and tomatoes, that she mentioned Magnus Jarrold.

'Pete and I have always wanted him to come over to see Tequila,' said Mandy, guiding Tory over to a corner of the room where some wicker armchairs were arranged. 'When Pete took over the island about ten years ago it was nothing but a fly-ridden swamp surrounded by beautiful beaches. He saw its possibilities, and by planting it with coconut palms and sea-grape trees, slowly reclaimed it from the mosquitoes. It was literally a desert island. Everything had to be provided —power, water, roads, a dock, communication,

86

housing. Now it's a dream come true—Pete's dream of a holiday resort where nice quiet people who work hard for their livings can unwind and relax.'

'It's amazing,' said Tory. 'And I'm sure Magnus would be interested to see what plants can achieve, but I'm surprised he's never talked about it to me.'

'Perhaps he doesn't look much beyond his own work,' replied Mandy shrewdly. 'He's always struck me as being one of those absent-minded professor types only interested in his own back yard.'

Tory subdued an urgent desire to defend Magnus and glanced across the room, where Denzil and Pete were leaning against the table, forking up food from their plates and talking seriously.

'Have you met Dr Jarrold?' she asked Mandy.

'No, I've only heard of him from Pete and friends of mine in Port Anne. I used to go to school with his wife, Rita Ribiera. It's my belief that Magnus Jarrold was given the job of Director of the Gardens because her father is a big name in the island. What's the news on Rita these days, by the way?'

The casual query chilled Tory's blood in the same way that Denzil's whispered question about Magnus's wife had chilled her the night before. Again she glanced at him, but he was talking to Pete and seemed to have no interest in herself or Mandy. Yet she could not help suspecting that the 'word' he had been so keen to have with Mandy had concerned Rita Jarrold, and had resulted in Mandy's question.

'What sort of news do you mean?' she asked as casually as she could, forking up some more of the delicious morsels of shrimp and lobster meat from her plate.

'About her health. You know she's in some fancy medical clinic in the States, taking treatment for suspected cancer of the throat? The last I heard she was making good progress and was expected home soon. I gather she hasn't returned yet.'

'No, she hasn't returned,' repeated Tory faintly, and leaned against the back of her chair. The food on her plate looked suddenly nauseous and she could tell by the taut feel of her skin that her face had gone pale.

'It developed while they were living in England,' Mandy went on in her deep lazy voice. 'The illness, I mean. That's why they came back to Airouna. It was thought that the English climate was making Rita ill when she kept getting sore throats and hoarseness, but after a few months back in the Caribbean it was realised, when her throat didn't seem any better, that the problem was more severe. Such a pity too, because she had a lovely singing voice.'

'Oh, I didn't know,' said Tory, finding that her own throat was dry and that her voice came out croakily. Mandy looked up and eyed her shrewdly, then rose to her feet.

'I'll get you another drink, honey,' she said in her languid way.

Alone, Tory picked at the remains of her food, hearing Pete's fat chuckle against the background of soft music coming from a tape deck. Rita Jarrold was alive; not very well it was true, but still alive, and would be returning to her home and husband on Airouna soon.

Her initial reaction was to think that Magnus had deceived her deliberately by withholding all information about his wife. Then her intelligence took over. No, Magnus was not to blame. She had deceived herself, wilfully, had been blinded to reality by her infatuation for him.

Mandy returned with a glass of fruit punch and this time it seemed to Tory that the rum content of the drink had been increased, but it eased her throat and she was able to finish her food and go to the table herself to select a succulent mango as dessert. No more mention was made of Rita Jarrold, and when they all returned to the verandah to lounge in the sea-cooled shade during the hottest part of the day, conversation dwindled away as they all slept or seemed to sleep.

The informal but much-needed siesta over, Tory went with Mandy to swim in the lagoon. She had expected Denzil to join them, but he went with Pete to the hotel area to meet some guests who were interested in chartering a yacht.

'You like Denzil?' Mandy enquired as they made their way back from the beach to the house.

'I hardly know him,' replied Tory evasively.

'Ho, hum,' laughed Mandy, and the swing of her elegant body as she entered the house seemed to express her scorn of the answer. 'You hardly know him, yet you and he kiss like lovers. I know because I watched you through the binoculars. I was surprised. I didn't know English people could be so demonstrative or so passionate.'

'Oh, we have our moments,' Tory returned lightly.

'And that was one of them?' Mandy turned to eye her curiously.

'No, that was a mistake.' Tory was suddenly angry because Denzil had put her in such a position. 'Oh, Denzil is a tormenting devil! Every time we meet he goes out of his way to tease me.'

'About Dr Jarrold?' queried Mandy, and Tory flashed her a wary glance.

'He told you how I feel about Magnus, didn't he?' she accused furiously. 'That was why he came ahead to talk to you before you met me. Oh, it's none of his business and he had no right to tell you. I ... I hate him for interfering!'

She knew she was behaving badly, yet she was unable to control herself because the shock of learning that

Rita Jarrold was alive, delayed by the siesta and the swim, was now having its way with her, making her want to vent her anguish and frustration on the person who had thought it necessary for her to face up to reality—Denzil.

'He did it because he cares,' said Mandy quietly.

'About me?' Tory was scornful now. 'Oh, come off it. He cares about no one but himself. He's unkind and inconsiderate.'

'Listen, honey, I know you're hurt and resentful, but you had to learn about Rita one day,' said Mandy, putting a comforting nurselly arm about Tory's shoulders and leading her to a divan-like settee to sit down. 'How you've managed to live for two months on Airouna without knowing about her is beyond me, but maybe like Dr Jarrold you can see no further than your own back yard. Rita is one of the few celebrities the island has produced, and we islanders are all very proud of her. Of course she's always performed under her maiden name of Ribiera.'

'Performed what?' asked Tory miserably.

'Songs, mostly Portuguese and Brazilian folk songs. You haven't heard her recordings with Pedro Lobos, the Brazilian guitarist?'

'No, I haven't.'

'Then you've missed something very special and unusual. When Pete comes back I'll ask him to play one to you. But to get back to your not knowing about her —hasn't Dr Jarrold ever talked about her?'

'A little, but you see ... oh, I know this will sound silly to you, but it seemed to hurt him to talk about her, so I thought she must have died and when he hesitated I said I understood. He seemed relieved that I did, and so ...'

'And so you deceived yourself, because you didn't want to hear that he had a wife with whom he might be in love because you were in love with him yourself,' finished Mandy gently. 'No, it doesn't sound silly to me. We're all guilty of self-deception in our lives at sometime or other, especially when we're young. Of course it hurt Dr Jarrold to talk about Rita because he's always been devoted to her. He met Rita when she was at a very low ebb after she'd been deserted by her first husband. Knowing of his devotion it's not surprising that relatives and friends of Rita were a little perturbed when you arrived on the island and went to live in his house, but then when you walked into the reception last night on his arm, looking radiant, so I'm told, the fat was in the fire. It was then that Denzil decided he had to do something about you.'

Tory sat slumped and silent, going over all that Denzil had said the previous night; his taunts about her bewilderment, about her being an innocent abroad. How right he had been!

'Why didn't he tell me about her?' she asked dully.

'Partly because he felt you wouldn't believe him, partly because last night's party wasn't the place; too many sharp eyes watching, you know, and partly because he didn't know much about Rita himself. But he knew I did, so he invited you to come today.' Mandy rose to her feet and went to the window to gaze out at the sea. 'Now that you know all, what are you going to do?' she asked.

'I don't know. I'll have to think about it,' replied Tory. 'Maybe I won't do a thing. Maybe I'll just wait until Mrs Jarrold returns.'

'Mmm. I wonder if that's wise?' murmured Mandy. 'Rita has an artistic temperament. She can't stand competition, and has a way of dealing with it quickly and effectively. She isn't going to be pleased to find you living in the same house.'

'But Magnus arranged for me to stay there because

there was nowhere else available for me to stay,' protested Tory. 'And I can't leave, because I'm under contract to work for a year and I don't want to break it. I'll just have to wait and see what happens.' She smiled rather tremulously. 'I'm not really afraid of Mrs Jarrold, you know, because I've done nothing I shouldn't. I've worshipped Magnus from afar, that's all. And I'd like you to know that I appreciate your telling me everything today, Mandy.'

The other woman turned to smile at her.

'And you won't take it out on Denzil for interfering?' she queried.

'Oh, Denzil,' said Tory with a sigh. 'He's another matter altogether. I don't think I'll ever be able to cope with him. He's a law unto himself.'

'Is that how you see him? As arrogant, domineering? Isn't it more true to say that he sees what should be done and does it? That he acts instead of hesitating or turning a blind eye? I don't know him very well, but I do know this, that Pete thinks the world of him, and that's enough for me,' said Mandy forcefully. 'And now I must get out of this swimsuit. I expect the men will be back soon and then it will be sundowners on the verandah. Ah, don't you love the way of life in the islands, Tory? Come day, go day and God sent Sunday, as my father used to say.'

But they didn't have sundowners on the verandah, because they went to the hotel dining pavilion for dinner with the guests who were interested in chartering a yacht. Mandy lent Tory a dress to wear which fitted not too badly because they were of similar height and since it was belted at the waist any surplus width could be disguised. Tory was glad of the diversion of the small social occasion because it prevented her from thinking about her own problems. It meant, too, that she could avoid direct conversation with Denzil; not that he made any effort to talk to her, being apparently more interested in making an impression on the daughter of the American businessman who wanted to charter a yacht, a long-limbed beauty with a gorgeous tan, sparkling blue eyes and, of course, masses of blonde hair.

Later, when the stars hung like huge clusters of diamonds in the black velvet of the sky and the frogs were croaking their monotonous chant they walked back to the de Freitas house. The tap-tap of *Ariel's* main halliard against the mast, the rustle of leaves and the smack of waves against sand and stone indicated that the night wind was strong.

'Where would you two like to spend the night?' Mandy asked in her casual way as they reached the path which led up to the house. 'You're welcome to sleep here.'

'I'll sleep on board,' Denzil answered crisply. 'I want to make sure the boat is anchored properly. Tory can please herself.'

Tory thought of the two berths in the small cabin, remembered the effects of propinquity and retreated.

'I'd like to sleep in the house, please,' she said stiffly, and to her annoyance Denzil laughed.

'Not in the mood for experiments tonight, Victoria?' he jeered. 'Oh, well, I can take a hint. See you in the morning.'

He went off in the direction of the jetty and Pete lumbered after him, saying that he'd help with the dinghy. Tory hesitated as she peered through the shadows, half-tempted to change her mind. Then she heard Denzil laughing again and resenting his mockery she turned quickly and followed Mandy to the house.

She slept badly even though the bed was comfortable, and several times during the night she wished she had gone with Denzil. Tormenting and infuriating he would probably have been, but he would have been company. She wouldn't have felt as alone as she did in this room while she reviewed over and over again her own behaviour and her own feelings.

She was hurt, Tory couldn't deny that. Anyone who had been living in a fool's paradise as she had been for the past two months, only to be shaken out of it, was bound to be hurt. But she couldn't make out whether she was hurt because she had discovered there was a possibility now that Magnus would never return her love or whether it was because she had a niggling feeling that he had deceived her by inviting her to live in his house without ever telling her of the existence of his wife.

Wasn't it possible that the pain she was feeling was disillusion because the man she loved and trusted, to whom she had devoted so much time, had betrayed that love and trust because he had failed to be honest with her, to square with her? Could she continue to love him knowing that he had a wife whom he loved? Was she the sort of person who could spend the rest of her days in selfless devotion to a man who didn't return her love?

She knew she wasn't. She knew she wanted a fulfilling relationship, the sort her parents had with each other, a sharing of everything, feelings, hopes, ambitions as well as all the physical things such as income and house, bed and board, an intimate warm partnership, even if she had to wait to achieve it.

Wait for what? For Rita Jarrold to die? Tory writhed on the bed. It was one thing to love a man whose wife had died, quite another to love a man whose wife was sick and might die. She couldn't and wouldn't let herself hope for that. And the possibility of Magnus ever divorcing Rita or her divorcing him seemed out of the question.

What, then, was the answer? How could she fulfil this silly hopeless love of hers for Magnus, if indeed it was love and not further self-deception? By a relationship outside his marriage? Was that where she was headed? Was that what he expected?

Tory sat up sharply in repudiation of the idea. She couldn't do it. Mind and body shrank in revulsion from it. Her head aching from introspection, she swung off the bed and went to the window. Dawn streaked the eastern sky with grey light, and down on the lagoon she could just make out *Ariel* riding to anchor, not moving on the mirror-like morning surface of the lagoon.

And as she stared the sunrise came with a sudden flushing of the sky. Round as a red ball the sun popped above the horizon. The sea became a deep rose-tinted blue, the lagoon changed from grey to a pale shimmering green. The yacht ceased to be a ghostly shape as the mast and varnish took on a golden gleam and the smooth white hull reflected the light flashed back to it from the water.

There was movement on board. A figure appeared in the hatchway, swung up into the cockpit and untied the rope which tied the dinghy to the stern of the yacht. Watching Denzil step into the dinghy, sit on the centre thwart and fit the oars into the rowlocks as it drifted away from the yacht, Tory felt a sudden urge to be with him. Turning from the window, she flung off the nightdress she had been lent by Mandy, stepped into her short shorts, pulled on her striped top, and carrying her bikini and her sailing shoes in her hand she tiptoed out of the room, along the passage to the front door, then opened it quietly and left the house.

CHAPTER FIVE

THE morning air was clear, giving everything, the curves of the coconut palms over the beach, the angle of the stone jetty, the scoop-shape of the small dinghy on the water, a sharp edge. At the end of the jetty Tory looked down into lucid water and saw thousands of tiny fish darting about in a world of sun-shot green light.

Shipping his oars and letting the dinghy drift a little, Denzil tilted his head back and looked at her from under the slant of his cap brim.

'You're up early,' he said, and the coolness of his voice was like a refreshing splash of water, alerting her to the fact that he was not feeling friendly this morning.

'I couldn't sleep,' she admitted.

'I'm not surprised,' he retorted. 'Mandy told you about Rita Jarrold, didn't she? And that would keep your mind on the hop all night.'

'How do you know it would?' she replied weakly.

'Think you're the only one who's been in this situation?' he countered enigmatically. 'You'd have been better on board the yacht with me, experimenting, than lying alone writhing.' He paused, eyeing her with an expectant gleam, obviously waiting for her to retaliate, but she was too tired to quarrel with him.

'I know. I kept wishing I'd gone with you,' she said in a low voice, and saw his eyebrows lift in satirical surprise. 'Denzil, do you think we could leave now and sail somewhere else before we go back to Airouna?'

By the way of answer he lifted the oars and rowed in towards the jetty. When the dinghy bumped against the stone he jumped ashore, tied the painter to an iron ring and then turned to face her. Raising a hand, he took hold of her chin to tilt her face to the light of the sun.

'Black lines under the eyes, a droop to the mouth— oh, you are in a bad way, Victoria,' he mocked. 'And you think that sailing all day might help?'

'Yesterday I felt free, without a care in the world, when we were sailing here,' she said. 'I'd like to feel like that again.'

'Escapist!' he jeered. 'Running away from the problem won't help. You and Jarrold have both tried that already, only you didn't run. You both buried your heads in the sand. Rita Jarrold is coming back, she's on her way now.'

'How do you know that?' she exclaimed.

'I was told on Friday night by one of the people I had dinner with, Ella Carson, who's in the know because she's secretary to Harold Ribiera, Rita's father. Your dear professor has gone to St Thomas to meet his wife to accompany her on the last part of her journey home.'

'Oh! He told me he was going to St Thomas to attend to some family business,' she said.

'He didn't lie. Rita *is* his family,' he pointed out dryly.

'Yes, I suppose she is,' Tory murmured dully, and again the nasty feeling of having been deceived niggled at her. Magnus could have been more honest, more straightforward in his dealings with her. 'Can we go sailing, Denzil?' she asked.

'You don't have to make the suggestion to me twice,' he replied with a touch of self-mockery. 'I'll go sailing at the drop of a hat. I'll just go up to the house to tell Pete we're off. Any message for Mandy?'

'Only to thank her for everything.'

Within half an hour *Ariel* was on her way south again, her sails full as she bounded over the white-crested blue sea. This time Denzil let Tory take the tiller, leaving her alone in the cockpit to steer while he went below to cook breakfast. She hadn't thought she was hungry, but she ate every scrap of the bacon and eggs he brought to her and gulped down several cups of tea. He didn't come into the cockpit to eat with her, but stayed in the cabin and later she could hear him talking into the ship-to-shore radio. But she didn't mind being left alone as long as she knew he was there, because in keeping the boat sailing, in sitting there feeling the fresh breeze on her skin and seeing the distant islands pop up to loom against the horizon, she found the forgetfulness of self and problems that she had sought all night.

As they cleared the southernmost tip of Tequila another island appeared, lying further to the west, and Denzil, who by that time was standing on the cabin roof attempting to take shots of the sun with his sextant, pointed to it.

'That's Berenique Island,' he shouted. 'Let's go there. There's a sheltered bay just west of the most northerly point. We could swim there, perhaps take a siesta.'

He freed the sheets so that she could alter course to run before the wind towards the distant hump. At once the motion of the yacht changed; no longer did it forge forward but rolled and pitched on the waves, and Tory had a hard time keeping the tiller in the right place, knowing that if she was not careful the yacht might gybe violently or broach to so that the waves, which were much higher than they had been the day before, might slop over into the cockpit and swamp the boat.

Since it was noon the sun's rays were hot and she was wearing the protective pyjama jacket as well as her sunhat. The movement of the boat plus the heat, added to the sleeplessness of the night before, had a soporific effect and several times she caught herself nodding and her eyes closing.

As they drew closer to the island she could see that it was higher than Tequila and was smothered by rain forest. Denzil took the tiller over the tip of a rocky point as he guided the boat past it and turned into a tiny bay with a crescent of silvery sand at its head.

Denzil luffed the boat within inches of the beach and when Tory dropped the anchor down from the bow at his command she watched it dig and hold in hard sand at the bottom of several feet of clear turquoise water.

Apart from the lapping sound of water against the hull of the boat and the occasional squawk of a parrot from among the dense vegetation that crowded down to the edge of the beach all was silent. As she moved lethargically to help Denzil furl the lowered mainsail round the boom, Tory felt sleepiness overwhelming her again. With a muttered excuse she left him and went down to the cabin. Within a few seconds of stretching out on one of the berths she was fast asleep.

She woke to the sound of the anchor chain dragging across the bottom and opened her eyes to blink at the white-painted ceiling of the cabin. Patterns of yellow light quivered on it, indicating that the sun was half way down the sky and peering in through the portholes. Turning her head, she saw Denzil sitting on the other berth, his legs thrust out before him, his arms folded across his chest, watching her with hard cold eyes.

'Sleep well?' he asked.

'Oh, yes.' Tory struggled to a sitting position. 'What time is it?'

'About four.'

'I slept so long?' she gasped.

'Like to go for a swim?' he suggested, and she nodded her agreement.

They swam from the boat, diving off the side-deck into the silky warm clear water and climbing back on board by way of a small ladder which hooked on to the side of the boat. Denzil produced snorkelling equipment and went off underwater while Tory sat and sunned herself, keeping a lookout for the tell-tale tube sticking above the water. The sleep had refreshed her, but her mind was still numb, closed to thought and feeling, and she was glad of Denzil's withdrawn attitude. He was there yet not there, silent yet supportive.

When he came back from his snorkelling expedition he had some fish, snappers he called them. He cooked them for their evening meal, which they ate on deck as the shadows grew long. Again they didn't talk much. She could have asked him about his sailing experiences, found out more about him, but she didn't. She didn't want to disturb the tranquillity of mood which had been produced by the beauty and peace of their present surroundings.

Sunset came, a vivid one which left orange streaks across a sky of pale primrose. The mainsail was hoisted, the anchor was pulled up and as the first stars pricked the darkening eastern sky, the yacht ghosted out of the small bay.

As they sailed in the dark, watching the brilliant glitter of stars above the dim shape of the mast, glancing over the side to see the glow of phosphorescence dancing in a wave, Tory was surprised to find herself feeling happy.

'I could sail like this for ever,' she said, and heard Denzil, who was a dark shadow in the opposite corner of the cockpit, laugh rather sceptically.

'Sailing isn't always like this,' he remarked.

'I realise that, but times like this must make up for

all the other difficult, hair-raising times when sky and sea are grey and the wind is roaring and you wonder if you'll ever survive,' she replied.

'Which is also a good description of life, don't you think?' he countered. 'There are moments which you wish could last for ever, moments when you feel completely content to be where you are and with the person who happens to be around at the time.'

Tory was silent for a few seconds as she realised with a little leap of surprise that part of her contentment now was because she was with him.

'My father says that if you can stand being at sea on a small boat with one person for a week, you can stand being with that person for the rest of your life. He put it to the test by going on a sailing cruise with my mother before he married her,' she said.

His chuckle was appreciative.

'He sounds like a man of good sense,' he remarked, and rose to his feet. 'Watch the compass. You're straying off course.'

'Oh!' She glanced guiltily at the illuminated compass which swung on a wooden box on a bar of wood that fitted across the cockpit. 'How do you know I am?'

'I can hear the foresail flapping and the wind hasn't changed,' he replied, and ducked down into the cabin, leaving her to the glimmer of stars in the clear dark sky, the chuckling sound of water under the bow, the creak of the mast and the wide expanses of heaving light-flecked water all about her, and her thoughts, which were suddenly alive and leaping as she wondered about Denzil and why he had concerned himself with her problems. Why had he interfered?

He did it because he cares, Mandy had said, *cares for people and tries to help when he sees help is required*. Well, he had certainly gone to a lot of trouble to make sure she learned about Rita Jarrold before the woman arrived home, thought Tory, and she could see now that it was as well that he had done so as her imagination leapt ahead to Magnus's return. How awful it would have been for her to be faced suddenly with his wife.

But why hadn't Magnus told her on Friday night that he would be bringing his wife home? The figures on the compass blurred slightly as the feeling she had been deceived by him surged up inside her again.

'Hey, watch it!' Denzil's voice was sharp. 'You're off course again.'

Tory blinked back the tears and tugged at the tiller with both hands to get the boat back on course and to stop the sails from flapping.

He came up, bringing two mugs of coffee and a tin of biscuits. He set the self-steering device and sat down beside her, a warm dark vibrant bulk against which she had a sudden longing to lean; a longing she discarded instantly as being weak and silly.

'You've started feeling again, haven't you?' he murmured. 'I can tell because you've stopped concentrating. Want to talk about it?'

'I ... it's just that I can't understand why Magnus didn't tell me he was going to bring her home,' she muttered.

'Perhaps he didn't think it was any of your business. After all, you did tell me once that it was all on your side and that he sees you only as his assistant,' he said dryly.

'Oh, I said that because I was annoyed with you,' she retorted.

'So there have been developments, have there?'

'Only small ones, but on Friday Magnus said he regards me as a friend.'

'And he kissed you, and even though nothing else happened you went to bed in a state of euphoria,' he mocked.

'No, I didn't, actually. I was a bit disappointed because ...' She broke off in consternation as she realised what she had been going to say—*Because I didn't feel as I feel when you kiss me.'*

'Because what?' he prompted, but when she didn't say anything he went on, 'It seems to me I was pretty near yesterday morning, when I suggested he hadn't come up to scratch. So what are you going to do now?'

'Go back to work at the Gardens. What else can I do? I'm under contract, remember.'

'And do you really think you're going to be allowed to stay in that house when Rita Jarrold is back?' Denzil exclaimed sharply, turning towards her. 'Good God, Tory, have you no knowledge of your own sex? When she hears what's been said about you and her husband, when she sees how attractive you are, do you really think she's going to believe you're innocent? She's either going to throw you out or make your life so damned uncomfortable that you'll want to leave. You're in one hell of a spot, but I don't suppose for one minute that you'll admit you've been placed in it by the lack of forethought, the sheer lack of caring either for you or his wife, by that dear professor of yours—who doesn't seem to care a damn about people as long as nothing interferes with his study of flowers and plants.'

His anger seemed to crackle about her like an electric storm. She couldn't understand why he was so angry, could think of nothing to say in defence of Magnus, and while she sat in confused silence Denzil heaved to his feet, climbed out of the cockpit and went up on to the foredeck.

Once more alone, Tory sat hunching herself in the anorak she was wearing as a protection against the coolness of the night wind. The lovely day was over, its tranquillity torn to shreds by the sharpness of Denzil's words, and as she thought back over what he had just

103

said, she could find only one word which had given her any pleasure. For the first time since she had met him he had called her Tory and not Victoria.

It wasn't long before the lights of Port Anne appeared on the port bow. Soon they were entering the bay, passing by the big red buoy whose light winked at them every six seconds. By lining up three red lights so that they appeared to be in a vertical line they found the entrance to the marina. Lights strung out along each pontoon were reflected in the almost still water, their shapes elongated so that they looked like Chinese lanterns.

Although it was late there were still people about, sitting on decks and in cockpits talking and laughing, enjoying the warm starlit night, and a few voices called out a greeting to Denzil as he and Tory made their way along the pontoon after they had left *Ariel* shipshape and tied up in her berth.

Since his angry outburst they hadn't said much to each other, and it was difficult to ignore the slight tension which existed between them. Tory had an impression that he'd had enough of her for one weekend. He had done what he felt he should do to help her, and now he wanted to shake her off, so she was surprised when he turned to her and said,

'You can stay the night with me if you like.'

They had reached the yard in front of the office building; the pale gravel glittered under the light shed from two powerful lamps which jutted out from the building. Tory looked up at his dark face, wishing she could read the expression in his eyes, but they were hidden by the shadow of his cap brim.

He was offering her an alternative to staying in a house where she might not be welcome any more, and for a moment she was tempted to accept his invitation. Then she remembered that there was only one bed in his bungalow. She remembered the force of propinquity and that hidden physical attraction they had for each other, and took fright.

'No ... no, thank you. I ... I have to go back. You see, Mrs Dunnet will be expecting me and ...'

'Okay, you don't have to make excuses,' he interrupted her curtly.

He turned on his heel and strode off towards the jeep, and by the time she caught up with him its engine was roaring. As soon as she was seated it shot forward towards the marina entrance.

Along the winding road they went, cutting corners dangerously. The tyres screeched on the surface of the road as they turned in through the elegant stone gateposts and gravel spat in all directions as they sped past the darkly shimmering pool. In front of the big house several parked cars glinted under the beams of the jeep's headlights when it came to an abrupt squealing stop.

'Oh, Magnus must be back,' Tory exclaimed, recognising the cream car.

'And you can guess what that means. Rita is back too,' drawled Denzil. 'Want to change your mind and come back to the bungalow with me?'

'Denzil, please don't think I'm not appreciative of all you've done for me this weekend,' she said in a low voice, 'but staying the night with you isn't going to solve anything, is it?'

'In my opinion staying the night with me would solve most of your problems,' he replied dryly. 'But I get the drift of the way you're thinking. You'd prefer not to share my bed. Okay, out you get, then. I'm not fond of long lingering farewells. Goodnight, Victoria.'

His cool dismissal of her hurt unexpectedly. It was like having a warm cloak that had been placed round her to protect her from an icy wind snatched away from her to leave her vulnerable and exposed. She hesitated, puzzled by her own reaction, and glanced sideways at him while she searched her mind for something conciliatory to say to him. But all she could see was his profile etched against the light coming from the house, the straight line of his forehead, the eagle curve of his nose, the arrogant jut of his chin, all as remote and uncommunicative as a painted portrait.

He revved the still running engine indicating that he was impatient to be gone, and with a muttered goodnight Tory was out of the jeep. She was still climbing the steps to the house when the vehicle left with a roar of the exhaust.

Inside the front door she paused. The sound of many voices, of laughter and music, came from the lounge, the door of which was open. A party was in progress! Tory made a rueful grimace and began to cross the hall to make her way to the back part of the house to tell Mrs Dunnet she was back. She did not have to go far because the woman came out of the kitchen, pushing before her a tea-trolley laden with cups and saucers, a coffee-pot and plates of savouries.

'What's happening, Mrs Dunnet?' Tory asked. 'Sounds like a party.'

'Dat's what it is, miss,' said the little woman. 'Mrs Jarrold is back home, the Lord be praised for his mercy, back home and as well as you or me.'

'When did she come?'

'Last night. Dr Jarrold brought her himself.'

'Mrs Dunnet, when you go in there, would you tell Dr Jarrold that I'm back, please?'

'I sure will, miss, I sure will.'

Tory went up to her room thinking that maybe when he knew she was back Magnus might come to have a word with her, to tell her his wife was back, perhaps even invite her to go down and join the party. If he did come, or sent a message by Mrs Dunnet, it would mean that he cared, and that Denzil had been wrong when he had suggested that Magnus cared neither for her or for his wife.

So she did not have a shower, but changed into a dress and sat down at the writing table to begin a letter to her parents describing her sail to Tequila. By the end of an hour, when neither Magnus nor Mrs Dunnet appeared, she admitted to herself that hoping he would come or send a message had been wishful thinking on her part, another little game of self-deception she had played with herself, and she went to bed.

She woke early next morning, dressed quickly and went downstairs to the dining room. To her relief Magnus was there alone. When he saw her he rose to his feet politely as he always did and greeted her in his usual vaguely pleasant manner.

'Good morning Tory. Did you have a good weekend?'

'Yes, thank you.' She had resolved to be bright and cheerful and not to show him that she was aware something unusual had happened. 'We sailed to Tequila on Saturday and spent the rest of the day there. It's really marvellous what Peter de Freitas has done with a mosquito swamp, using coconut palms and sea-grape trees. You should go and see it.'

She helped herself to fresh fruit salad from a bowl on the sideboard, poured coffee into a cup and carried everything to her place opposite to him.

'Yes, I suppose I should go over some time,' Magnus murmured. He picked up his cup, gulped some coffee quickly as if he hoped to derive some courage from it, and patted his mouth with his serviette which he then rolled into a tight roll and slipped into a silver ring. 'Tory ... I have something to tell you,' he added.

'When I flew to St Thomas on Saturday it was to meet my wife and bring her home.'

'I know,' she said calmly, looking up and directly at him.

The expression of relief which passed across his boyish features was almost ludicrous.

'Thank God for that,' he muttered. Then looking up and across at her he smiled, that wry diffident slant of the lips which she had once found so attractive and disarming. 'You see, I wasn't sure whether you knew about Rita. On Friday night at that reception some-one said ...' He paused and rubbed at his creased fore-head with his fingers, obviously troubled about what he had to say next, but for once Tory's heart didn't soften and she didn't rush to help him. She had learned the folly of doing that.

'Yes, Magnus, somebody said what?' she prodded him. A dull disfiguring red crept up over his face.

'It was suggested that possibly you weren't aware that Rita would be returning here to live,' he said in a low, slightly embarrassed voice.

'I didn't know,' she replied coolly, giving him a straight look which he avoided by sliding the serviette out of its ring, re-rolling it and pushing it through again. 'I didn't know your wife was alive, even. You could have told me on Friday evening when you said you were going to St Thomas.'

'Yes, well ... er ... you see, Tory, I thought you knew about Rita when you said you understood the first night you were here. And then on Friday I wasn't too sure I'd be meeting her. Everything happened so quickly. At the reception her father said he'd heard from her and that she wanted me to go to St Thomas and wait there as she hoped to be able to leave the clinic. I'd no idea that she would be there already.'

'I see,' she replied dryly.

'Tory.' Magnus leaned forward across the table and stretched out a hand to touch hers as he had on Friday night, but she moved her hand back and picked up her coffee cup. 'The fact that Rita is back won't make any difference to us. We'll go on in the same way as before ...' He broke off and his eyes widened as he looked past her. Slowly he rose to his feet and walked round the table towards the door.

'Rita, my dear! There was no need for you to get up so early. Surely you should stay and rest in bed as long as you can,' he said urgently, rather fussily.

Turning in her chair so that she could see who was entering the room, Tory was in time to see Magnus kissing the cheek of a slim dark-haired woman of about forty years of age.

'But I wanted to have breakfast with you, darling,' she said in a low husky voice. She looked across the room at Tory. 'And I also wanted to meet your assistant before you both went off to work.'

Slowly she walked across the room. She was in a brown linen suit and had a pimento-pink scarf tied round her throat. Her shoes matched the scarf perfectly. Her shoulder-length, sleek black hair curved about her olive-skinned face in a way that emphasised the hollows in her cheeks. Above the high cheekbones set under fine arching eyebrows her slanting eyes were black, opaque.

'Hello, Miss Latham, I'm Rita Jarrold. I've been looking forward to meeting you. I've heard so much about you and about your devotion to my husband from my daughter Carla.'

The tone of Rita's voice was pleasant. No one listening could have detected any malice in it. It was the choice of words and the sudden gleam in the dark eyes which conveyed the real message.

'And I've been looking forward to meeting you, Mrs

Jarrold,' replied Tory, feeling inwardly grateful to Denzil and Mandy for preparing her for this meeting. 'Especially since I've heard a record of your singing.'

'Oh?' The beautiful face expressed pleased surprise. Like most artistic celebrities Rita Jarrold was not immune to flattery. 'And where did you hear it?'

'At the home of an old school friend of yours, Mandy de Freitas.'

'You've been to Tequila, then?' Rita slid into a place at the table and Magnus set a cup of coffee down in front of her. 'Which record was it?'

'It was one from an album you recorded with Pedro Lobos.'

'And that was the first you've ever heard?' queried Rita. 'Magnus has never played any of his collection to you?'

'No.' The question made Tory uneasy. She could not help looking at Magnus for some sort of guidance, but he was either deliberately ignoring her glance of appeal or he wasn't listening to the conversation, because he made no remark. 'Dr Jarrold and I . . .' Tory tried to continue, but faltered to a stop.

'You meet only to work,' put in Rita quickly, 'but of course you do. I am glad you enjoyed the record. Unfortunately my singing days are over.'

'I'm sorry,' mumbled Tory.

'But everything has its bright side. Now I shall have all the time in the world to devote to being a good wife to Magnus. Darling, won't you have some more coffee?' Rita turned to Magnus with a smile which showed her almond-shaped teeth.

'No, thank you, I must get down to the lab. I'll see you there later, Tory. I'll be back for lunch, my dear.' He bent and kissed Rita on the cheek. 'Now don't overdo things, please.'

'I promise,' said Rita.

He left the room quickly as if glad to be gone from an awkward situation. Tory finished her coffee, wiped her mouth with her serviette and, excusing herself, stood up.

'One moment, Miss Latham.' The husky voice held a sharp note of command. 'There's no need for you to rush quite so precipitately after my husband. A little more discretion in your behaviour would be appreciated by me.'

Tory put a hand on the back of the chair she had just vacated. She felt she was going to need its support.

'I'm afraid I don't know what you mean,' she said, returning the inimical gaze of the black eyes.

'I mean, Miss Latham, that I know what's been going on behind my back during the past few months. I mean that I take exception to your obvious affection for Magnus. I mean that I object to your presence in this house and want you out of it as soon as possible.'

'Mrs Jarrold, you're quite mistaken,' Tory flared, her temper roused by the arrogance of the other woman. 'Nothing has been going on behind your back. I admit I'm fond of Magnus, but . . .'

'You really expect me to believe you when my own daughter, who has been here all the time, has told me of the hours you and Magnus have spent together in the evenings after working hours—either closed in his study or sitting on the terrace or walking in the gardens, when he neglected her to be with you?'

The husky voice was broken by a spasm of coughing.

'But, Mrs Jarrold, we were working, discussing his book and planning chapters and layout. Oh, please don't talk any more, you're straining your throat. You'll be ill again,' cried Tory.

'And would you care if I was? Would Magnus?' demanded Rita in a hoarse whisper. 'Oh, no, you can't expect me to believe that, or anything else you say.

I've heard all about your entrance to the reception on Friday night. My father told me, and this morning with my own ears I heard Magnus saying to you that my return would make no difference to you and him, that you'd go on as before.'

'But he didn't mean what you're thinking. He was referring to the book, I swear he was,' protested Tory.

'No, he wasn't. You see, Miss Latham, I know Magnus much better than you do. I know this strange attraction he has for young women who are looking for someone to care for. They fall for that diffident, helpless manner of his. Don't think for one moment this is the first time it has happened. When he was working in the States there was a little lab technician who couldn't do enough for him. I was away on tour at the time. When I returned I found her cooking for him, doing his washing—I leave you to guess what the next step was going to be. Something similar happened when he was appointed to a position in Copenhagen, and when we were in England I guessed that there was someone who took up his time, and you'll be surprised to learn that once I saw you both coming out of a tea-shop in the High Street. But I was ill and a change of climate was thought necessary, and it didn't take much to persuade him to accept the position of the Directorship here, in the island where I was born. But it wasn't possible for me to stay. I had to have treatment. I'd been gone only six months when I heard he had a new assistant ... one he didn't really need.'

'Mrs Jarrold, I'm sorry, I had no idea,' said Tory earnestly. 'Honestly.'

The dark eyes appraised her narrowly and insolently.

'Do you know, I could almost believe you. It must be the blonde hair, the wide clear eyes, the soft skin which make you appear so innocent. But I don't believe you. I've squared with you, Miss Latham, told you exactly how I feel, and in return I expect you to square with me. I give you until Wednesday night to leave this house, to find other lodgings. If you're not gone by then I shall see to it that your contract as a government employee is cancelled and that you find it difficult to obtain work of a nature suited to your qualifications and abilities elsewhere by making sure you are given poor references. Is that clear?'

'Yes, very clear, Mrs Jarrold.'

Tory turned away and almost collided with Carla, who was standing behind her listening to all that had been said. The girl grinned maliciously and Tory had the impression she would have liked to make a rude grimace, only the presence of her mother prevented her.

As she ran up the stairs to her room it occurred to her that Carla could have been responsible for Rita's sudden return. The girl had possibly carried tales to Lise Campos, possibly to her grandfather, to get her own back on Tory for being turned away from the marina.

Feeling sweat break out on her body because she had moved too quickly for the heat of the day, Tory went straight to the bathroom to clean her teeth, her mind echoing with some of Carla's more caustic comments. *You're sweet on my father. Why don't you take your own advice before you're taken advantage of?*

Oh, how blind she had been, how foolish, far worse than Carla who at least had known that Denzil wasn't married. And Carla had had the advantage that Denzil was a person who cared about people, who had the courage to be cruel to be kind so that when he had realised what was happening he had sent Carla packing. Whereas she had been led on by Magnus; not deliberately, but, because he was ineffectual, helpless and incapable of being unkind, he was actually more cruel.

And now she was faced with Rita's ultimatum. Find alternative lodgings or else ... She couldn't let the contract be cancelled. She had to be loyal to herself in this instance as well as loyal to her employers. But where could she stay? She was quite prepared to believe that Magnus had been telling her the truth when he had told her that good, reasonably priced lodgings were difficult to obtain. There were a couple of hotels in Port Anne, but to live in them all the time might prove expensive, and she would have to find some form of transport.

She took the problem to work with her and during the day asked the other assistant botanists and some of the gardeners, all of whom lived in bungalows on the botanical estate or nearby, if any of them knew where she could rent room and board. But none of them were able to help her. She decided not to approach Magnus, as she realised with a terrible feeling of disillusionment that he wouldn't be able to help her. She didn't even bother to tell him what had passed between herself and Rita. Let him continue to believe that his wife's presence in the house would make no difference, and that things would go on as before. Let him be shocked into awareness of reality as she had been, Tory thought with a touch of spite.

Then she felt pain twinge within her. How easily her feelings about Magnus had changed! How quickly she had fallen out of love with him once she had learned the truth about him. Her first love affair was over, and looking back on it Tory could see now that it had been a very adolescent, one-sided affair. She had been in love with an image and not with a real person at all.

Some idea of the difference the return of Rita Jarrold was going to make to the situation in the Director's house was made very clear that evening. When Tory went downstairs for the usual sundowners on the terrace she was intercepted by Mrs Dunnet, who informed her that the Jarrolds had company for dinner and that she was to take her meal in the small room off the kitchen. Later, when she decided to go into Port Anne to search for accommodation, instead of borrowing the cream car to drive herself in she had to phone for a taxi to come out and pick her up. She asked the grinning cheerful taxi-driver if he knew of any house where she might find a room. He gave her two addresses and left her outside one, but one glance at its seedy appearance and the rough-looking men who were hanging about outside and she knew that she would have to be in dire straits to even consider it.

She did eventually find a room in a pleasant clean house overlooking the bay, only to receive a phone call on Wednesday afternoon to say that the owner of the house had changed her mind. In desperation, because she had only a few hours in which to find somewhere to live, Tory went to tell Magnus the state of affairs.

'I'll have a word with Rita, my dear,' he promised, looking very worried. 'I'm sure she'll understand when I tell her how important it is to my work that you stay. I mean, how am I going to finish that book on time without your help? She can be very difficult at times and gets the most peculiar ideas. For instance, she believes that you and I have been having an affair. Anyway, leave it with me. I'm sure it will be all right for you to stay another night when I explain to her.'

So she had left it to him, and now she was sitting in her room trying to finish the letter to her parents which she had started on Sunday night after once again eating alone in the poky little room off the kitchen. The atmosphere was sultry and outside everything was still. Not a leaf rustled, not a frog croaked in the darkness beyond the window, and she guessed from past experience that a storm was brewing.

A knock at her door surprised her and she opened it

to find Rita standing there, looking elegant in a dark red evening gown which swathed her slim body. Her straight dark hair was swept up on top of her head and long golden earrings dangled from her earlobes.

'I'm surprised to find you still here,' she said, walking straight into the room and looking round it as if searching for damage to the walls or the furniture. 'You're supposed to have left by tonight. Is it possible that you want that contract torn up?'

Her dark glance came down from a survey of the ceiling to stare at Tory.

'No, I don't. Hasn't Magnus told you? He said he would have a word with you. I thought I'd found alternative lodgings, but this afternoon I had word that the landlady had changed her mind.'

A faintly malicious smile curved Rita's full lips.

'Yes, I'd heard about that,' she murmured smugly. 'The woman phoned here for references. I told her that I considered you to be untrustworthy. Magnus did mumble something about it being important to his work that you be allowed to stay on and I told him I had nothing against you as a botanist—I daresay you're very clever—but I don't want you living in this house. Now come along, get your things packed. We're going into Port Anne to visit my father. We could drop you off at one of the hotels.'

Tory discovered that she was trembling with the effort to control the anger which was surging up inside her.

'No, thank you,' she said coldly. 'I prefer to find my own way there.'

'Well, just be sure you're gone by the time we return at about ten o'clock, won't you?' Rita's glance swept once more over the room. 'This is really a very pleasant room. I think we might have it redecorated for Carla. The room she's in doesn't have its own bathroom. Goodnight, Miss Latham.'

She left the room and for a few minutes Tory stood, face buried in her hands as she tried once again to control the shakiness which swept over her. Never had she felt so humiliated. Never had she expected to come up against such relentless malice and hate, and considering Rita's recent remarks, she realised that not only did Rita want her out of the house, she also wanted her off the island, and that any attempts on her part to find lodgings were going to be blocked by the woman.

Gradually the shakiness passed, leaving her numb. She got out her cases and began to pack them, not caring very much how she threw the clothes in, wanting only to leave the house as fast as she could. While she was packing she heard the leaves begin to rustle as a wind shook them, but there was no relief from the humid heat which only seemed to increase until it pressed against her skin like something tangible, causing her to sweat at every movement.

She changed into slacks and a cotton blouse, pulled on her anorak and lugged the heavy suitcases downstairs. By now the wind had increased in violence and she could hear it moaning. In the hallway the electric light flickered once or twice as the overhead cables swung in the wind and tugged at their poles. Tory was looking through the small telephone directory for the number of a taxi service when the light went out altogether. Repeating the number she had found to herself so that she did not forget it, she groped for the instrument and picked up the receiver. A nasty buzzing noise indicating that the line was out of order came through the ear-piece, and as she replaced the receiver Tory could not help smiling ruefully. Even her efforts to leave the house under her own steam were being thwarted by natural causes!

By this time she expected Mrs Dunnet to appear with the usual candles which were put into use whenever the power failed. Then she remembered that Wednesday was the woman's evening off. Sitting down on a chair near the telephone table, she considered her next move, and peered at her watch to try to make out the time from its luminous dial, hearing the wind increasing in violence. She judged she had two hours before the Jarrolds returned and she didn't think that either the telephone or the electricity would be back in service by then. Experience of two previous tropical storms during her stay on the island warned her that such services would not be back in working order until two or three days after the storm was over, because of the islanders' easy-going attitude to work.

The only way she could get to Port Anne tonight would be by walking, and she couldn't walk the eight miles with two heavy suitcases, so she would leave them to be picked up later. Her decision made, Tory stood up, slung her canvas holdall which contained her nightwear and her handbag over her shoulder, opened the front door and stepped out of the house.

The darkness was complete, a black void in which trees and bushes swished and groaned. Wishing she had a flashlight, Tory went down the steps and set off in the direction of the entrance to the Gardens. She was skirting the pool, keeping a wary eye on where she was going in case she stepped into it, when the rain came in big spots, pinging down on broad leaves and hitting the water of the pool in a steaming hiss. Quickly she pulled the hood of her anorak over her hair which was already tangled by the wind, and ran for shelter beneath one of the tulip trees.

It wasn't pleasant standing there listening to the branches thrashing above her, and she soon left shelter to plunge through the stinging darkness across the lawn in the direction of the path that went over the hill to the marina, thinking she would cut at least five miles off her journey by taking the short cut.

The path was fast turning into a stream. Slithering and sliding in the mud, Tory managed to gain level ground and began to feel her way along the tunnel woven from vines and ferns. The foliage was so thick that rain scarcely penetrated, and it was so dark that she had to walk with her hands stretched out before her to save herself from walking into tree-trunks or being clouted by low-hung branches and vines. Several times she tripped and fell to her knees, always getting to her feet hastily because she did not like the feel of the ground beneath her hands, sure that once she had touched something slimy that moved.

Soon the enveloping darkness began to have a claustrophobic effect on her. She imagined the trees were closing in on her, and only just restrained a screech of horror when leaves touched her face with a stealthy lingering caress. She felt panic rising within her. She should never have come this way, she should have gone by the road. She might never get out of this tangle of sinister wet branches and leaves that would eventually twine themselves about her and choke her to death.

Panic took over and she began to run. Her foot turned on a rock or a root, she had no way of knowing which, and sharp pain stabbed through her ankle and up her leg, making her cry out. Standing on one foot with her eyes squeezed tightly closed and her teeth gritted together, she waited for the pain to recede, then cautiously put the injured foot to the ground. Pain was still there, but dulled now, and Tory was able to hobble onwards, feeling relief surge through her as she saw a greyness ahead which meant she was almost at the end of the tunnel.

Slowed down as she was by the twisted ankle, it took her almost as long to reach the end of the tunnel as it had to come from the tulip tree to the point where her foot had turned, but at last she emerged and looked down through the slanting rain at the dazzle of light at the marina.

How like Denzil to have a generator to supply emergency power, she thought as she limped down the path to the road. There she paused and looked along the road in the direction of Port Anne. Its surface gleamed wetly and she could hear the culverts at its side gushing noisily with the water which had run off the hill into them. Slowly she moved forward and pain exploded from the ankle, jarring her to a stop.

It was foolish to attempt to walk to Port Anne now. There was nothing else for it but to go to Denzil and ask him if she could use his phone, or if it was out of order, ask him to drive her into Port Anne.

CHAPTER SIX

FEELING drained of all energy, her nerves nagged by the pain of her twisted ankle, Tory went up the steps to Denzil's bungalow, using the wooden handrail to drag herself up. She pulled back the outer screen door and knocked with her knuckles on the closed front door. She waited for a while, listening. Faintly, below the sounds of rushing water and wind she could hear the bass accompaniment to music which she could not hear coming through the open window. No one came to the door so she knocked again, harder.

A few seconds later the door was opened by Denzil. He was wearing only white cotton trousers belted low on his hips; his feet were bare and his hair was tousled and there was a heaviness about his eyes which indicated that he had either been asleep or thoroughly relaxed when she knocked.

'Well, look what the high tide has washed ashore,' he drawled jibingly, and his hostility hit Tory like a blow. He made no attempt to invite her in or to move back so that she could enter, and she wondered suddenly if he had company.

'I hope I'm not disturbing you,' she said stiffly, but her attempt to appear coolly controlled was spoilt by the chattering of her teeth.

'Not really. I was just having a nightcap and writing a letter to my grandmother.' Her face must have expressed scepticism, for he added with a glint of mockery, 'I do have a grandmother. She's a very rich old lady and I have to keep in with her so that one day she'll leave me all her loot in her will.'

'I wish you wouldn't say things like that about yourself!' It burst out of her uncontrollably, surprising her as much as it surprised him.

'Why shouldn't I?' he countered.

'It might make people think you're nothing but a pirate, only doing things for your own profit, and you're not like that, you're not like that ...' Her voice rose and cracked a little hysterically, so she put her hands over her mouth to stop the words that seemed to want to babble out.

His eyes narrowed and his glance swept over her down to her muddy feet.

'My God,' he said softly. 'I believe you have been in the tide.'

'No, I haven't, I walked over the hill. Oh, it was horrible! I'll never do it again in the dark.' She lost control then and began to shake, burying her face in her hands. She had come to him instinctively for help and his derisive, hostile attitude had shattered her control completely.

She was vaguely aware of him pulling her indoors, of the door closing. Pain shot up her leg from her ankle. She winced and cried out.

'Now what's wrong?' he demanded.

'I twisted my ankle. My foot turned on a rock,' she muttered, and took her hands from her face to look round the room. There was no one else there.

'You deserve more than a twisted ankle for even attempting to come through the forest in a storm. Have you no sense at all?' he rapped, and gave her a sharp shake. The harshness of his voice and the roughness of the shake jolted Tory. She took a long sighing breath and gripped her hands together.

'It isn't as far as coming round by the road,' she explained. 'It's a long way to Port Anne, and ...'

'You decided to walk to Port Anne in that storm?' Denzil interrupted her incredulously. His fingers were busy with the cord which tied the hood of her anorak, trying to unknot it. 'Now I know you're crazy, stark raving bonkers,' he added with a sort of gentle mockery that assured her that his attitude had changed. He was no longer hostile.

'It was the only way I could get there. The electricity went off and the phone was out of order,' she continued with her explanation.

'Couldn't you have waited until the storm was over?' he asked, pulling the cord loose and pushing the hood back off her tangled hair.

'No. You see . . .' The job of having to explain about Rita took on enormous proportions which were beyond Tory's present capabilities. She began to shake again, and stood mutely while he unzipped the anorak and peeled it off her to drop it on the floor and pull her into his arms.

'Calm down, lover,' he said softly, holding her close against his warm bare chest. 'You're going to have a hot bath to wash all that mud off while I see what I can find in the way of clothing for you—a repeat performance of your first visit here.'

'I . . . I have some clothes with me . . . in my holdall,' she mumbled into his shoulder.

'You don't have a holdall with you unless it's on the steps outside,' he replied quietly.

'Oh, I remember now! I dropped it when I fell in the forest. I . . . I couldn't find it . . . it was so dark. Oh, Denzil, I've never been so frightened in my life . . .'

'Okay, okay. It's over now. You're here.'

An arm round her shoulder, he helped her to hobble to the bathroom. He made her sit on the chair while he put the plug in the bath and turned on the taps. When the bath was half full he felt the water with his hand, turned off the cold tap and let the hot run some more. Then he turned off both and turned to her.

'Can you manage now, or would you like me to stay in case you fall?' he asked coolly.

'I'll manage, thank you very much,' she said.

'I'll get you something to wear,' he murmured. 'Don't lock the door.'

Alone, Tory stripped slowly, becoming aware as she did so of the tattered state of her slacks and of the numerous scratches not only on her legs, but on her arms and face too. Shakily she hopped to the bath and stepped into it. The warm water was like balm to her shaking limbs and she lay back in the steam, half dazed by nervous reaction. She was still lying there half-submerged when Denzil returned. He dropped an article of clothing on the chair and his eyes glinted down at her through the steam.

'That's all I can find.' He bent and picked up her wet clothing and bundled it under his arm. 'Come into the living room when you're ready.'

He had gone before she had time to object to his cool invasion of her privacy, but in a way she was glad that she had been too surprised to speak because if she had she might only have roused his mockery, and she didn't want to do that. She wanted him to take over, to use his cool managing mind on her behalf, to comfort and protect her, and in return she would do anything for him, anything.

She was alarmed at her own admittance that she needed Denzil, possibly far more than he needed her. Somehow it seemed like surrender to a force against which she had been struggling for some time. Stepping out of the bath, she towelled herself and pulled on the man's beach robe he had brought. It was made from striped towelling and was too wide, but because it was only knee length for him it came to calf length on her, and since it had a tie belt she was able to wrap it round herself and secure it with the belt. With shaky fingers

124

she turned back the too long sleeves, then combed her hair with a comb on the shelf above the wash basin.

Knuckles slithered perfunctorily over the panels of the door, it was opened, and Denzil looked round it.

'Just making sure you're okay,' he explained laconically. 'Leave the mess, I'll clear it up later. I've made a drink for you.'

In the living room, shaded table lamps shed pools of mellow light and the blue and green striped curtains were pulled across the wide windows to shut out the wet darkness of the night.

Tory sat, or was rather gently pushed, down on to the big settee. She still felt dithery and when Denzil came back from the kitchen with a mug from which steam rose and handed it to her, she couldn't take it because she was afraid she wouldn't be able to hold it. At once he squatted before her so that his face was on a level with hers.

'Listen, my darling,' he said gently, and she knew he was using the endearment in the same way as he used *lover*, in the way the people from his part of England always used such words when they wanted to comfort or reassure. 'You're suffering from some kind of nervous shock and this drink will help you to relax, take the edge off things for a while. Come on, now, take a sip. It's mostly hot milk.'

It was a long time since she had been given hot milk to drink. It was something she always associated with being ill as a child, when her mother had cosseted her, putting her to bed with an aspirin taken with hot milk.

'I don't think I can hold the mug, my hands are shaking so much,' she murmured.

'Then I'll hold it for you.' He held the mug to her lips and she took a sip. 'More,' he insisted, so she took a big swallow. The milk had a strange tangy taste to it and she glanced at him suspiciously.

'What's in it?' she demanded.

'Rum,' he said, and smiled. She liked the way he smiled, Tory thought. She liked the way one corner of his mouth turned down while the other turned up. 'Rum and hot milk is my grandmother's cure for everything. She says that's why she's lived so long. She drinks it every night before she goes to bed.'

She took another sip. The smooth yet fiery liquid slipped down easily, and she could feel its warmth spreading through her body.

'You can hold it now,' said Denzil, taking one of her hands and pressing the fingers round the handle of the mug. 'It'll give me a chance to finish my own drink.'

Liking the ease that the drink had brought her, Tory sipped more of it, and felt the cushion beneath her sink as Denzil sat down beside her. Glass in hand, he leaned back and put his free arm along the back of the settee behind her.

'Like to tell me why you were hiking to Port Anne on a night like this?' he asked casually.

'I couldn't stay in that house any longer.'

'Because you didn't want to or because someone told you to clear out?'

'Both. You were right. Rita Jarrold told me to leave the first day. She gave me until tonight to find alternative accommodation. If I didn't, she said she would see that my contract would be torn up and that I wouldn't be able to find another job easily because of bad references.'

'Have you found alternative accommodation?'

'I thought I had, but this afternoon the woman who had offered me lodgings told me she'd changed her mind. I asked Magnus if he could persuade his wife to give me more time. I don't know if he did or not, but tonight she came to my room and ordered me to pack.

They were going out for the evening and she said that if I hadn't gone by the time they returned she'd act … Oh, she's been horrible and vindictive. She's spreading lies about me, telling people I'm untrustworthy. She's humiliating me.'

The shame and the shock of all that had happened to her since Monday rose up and burst out. Sobs shook her and tears ran down her face. Denzil took the mug from her hand and set it on the floor with his own glass, then put his arms round her and pulled her against him. She lay with her head on his chest. He didn't say anything, but she felt his hand smoothing her arm under the sleeve of the robe and gradually her sobs subsided. It was good to be held by him, she thought hazily, to feel the solid support of his body, the warm hairiness of his skin beneath her damp cheek, the hardness of bone and muscle against her softness, the tender lingering caress of his hand on her arm. She would like to lie against him all night, to go to sleep like that comforted and protected, but she had to get to Port Anne.

'Denzil, may I use your phone?' she asked, and found that it was difficult to talk because all of a sudden her tongue felt thick and didn't want to form the words. So she tried again, speaking slowly, making an effort to be distinct. 'Denzil, may I use your phone?'

'It's out of order, like the one you tried to use earlier,' he replied lazily.

'Oh dear!' Tory wanted to giggle because nothing seemed to be working. 'I have to get to Port Anne. I have to book a room in a hotel, but I can't walk there because I've hurt my ankle, so will you please take me in your jeep?'

'No.'

He didn't want to help her after all, she thought miserably. And she had thought he would be on her side. She raised her head. It seemed very heavy and everything seemed to whirl around her. She glared at him through the tangle of hair that fell across her face.

'Why not?' she demanded.

'Because your clothes are in a mess and I haven't anything else but that beach robe for you to wear. Right now it isn't exactly decent.'

'Oh!' She glanced down and found that the robe was gaping at the front. She pulled one edge of the robe over the other tightly to close the opening, tossed the hair back out of her eyes and encountered his twinkling, derisive eye.

'You have the most wicked glint in your eyes whenever you look at me, Denzil Hallam,' she accused.

'You know, Victoria, I think the rum has gone to your head and that I'd better put you to bed,' he retorted with a grin.

'Which bed?' she asked, frowning at him. There was no doubt her head was behaving in a most peculiar way, and she longed to lay it on his shoulder again.

'My bed. There is no other bed,' he replied, and began to shift forward with the intention of standing up. She reached out and caught his arm.

'Can't I sleep here, in your arms?' she pleaded.

'Much as I'm flattered by the fact that you want to sleep in my arms, I think you'd be more comfortable in bed. Come on, up you get,' Denzil ordered, rising to his feet and holding a hand out to her. She took it and he pulled her to her feet. Pain twinged agonisingly in Tory's ankle, the room whirled about her and she had to hold on to him.

'I'd forgotten about the ankle,' he murmured, and lifted her easily in his arms. Glad that he had taken over again, she put her arms round his neck and nestled her head against his shoulder.

In the bedroom he set her on her feet, pulled back the coverings on the bed and pushed her down on to it. Dizzily she lay back against the pillow as he lifted her legs on to the bed and covered her with the sheet and thin blanket. He turned away and she felt suddenly desolate, a great fear of being left alone swamping her so that she reached out and caught his hand.

'Denzil, please don't leave me by myself all night,' she pleaded. 'Please stay with me.'

'Okay,' he replied, calmly reassuring. 'I'll stay. I'll be back in a few minutes.'

Reassured, she let go his hand and closed her eyes. The pillow was comfortable, the sheets were cool and she seemed to be floating in a circle, round and round and round, so she turned on to her side.

She must have slept, for she knew nothing more until she felt a movement behind her. Opening her eyes to darkness, she thought she was back in the tunnel of trees coming over the hill and that some monster was moving behind her, coming closer, actually grasping her round the waist. Turning quickly, she put out her hands to fend it off. Her hands touched bare skin, felt the hardness of bone, moved upwards to encounter the roughness of hair.

'If you're going to persist with this sort of behaviour I hope you're prepared to take the consequences,' Denzil whispered mockingly, his arm tightening about her.

'Oh, I thought you were a monster,' she exclaimed, and snatched her hands away.

'No, I'm merely a man, one with vigorous appetites,' he retorted dryly. 'Judging by your reaction it seems you'd prefer to find yourself with a monster, so why don't you turn over? It'll be safer for both of us if you do. You're still a little squiffed.'

Tory did as he suggested, but he kept his arm about her and drew her close into the curve of his body, and she fell asleep at once, feeling warm and secure.

When she wakened again sunlight was warm on her face. She was on her back and something heavy was lying across her chest. There was a faint feeling of discomfort in the region of her head, as if her hair was being pulled. Turning her head, she saw that Denzil was beside her, apparently fast asleep, his face half buried in a swathe of her hair which lay on the pillow. The weight on her chest was his arm.

She frowned, trying to remember how she came to be in this bed with him lying beside her, but all she could recall was being in the living room drinking hot milk. She glanced at him again, noting how calm his face appeared in sleep. His lashes were thick and dark against his cheek and there were fine laughter lines fanning out from the corners of her eyes. His dark hair had golden glints in it, as did the fine dark down which covered the forearm resting across her.

Suddenly she didn't want him to be asleep. She wanted him awake and aware of her. She wanted his eyes to glint wickedly at her, his arm to tighten around her and draw her close. She wanted to feel his mouth, hard and passionate, against hers. She wanted the fire of his passion to touch her and rouse a similar feeling within her.

Her fingers trailed caressingly up his arm over the curve of his bare shoulder. There her hand lingered as if to soak up the pleasure the feel of skin over firm muscle gave her. Slowly she stroked the line of collarbone to his throat, then curled her hand round to the back of his neck. As he moved his head a little in response to her touch, turning so that he was face to face with her, she leaned forward and touched his lips with hers, then drew away and watched.

His eyelids lifted, his eyes gleamed at her briefly, then were covered again.

'Denzil?'

'Mmm.'

'Have you been here all night?'

'Yes. You didn't want to be left alone,' he murmured, his eyes still closed.

'I can't remember anything. What did you put in that drink?'

'Only rum, too much for an innocent like you, apparently.' He chuckled sleepily and settled his head more comfortably against her hair. 'I had to carry you in here and later you dreamt a monster was chasing you.' He opened his eyes suddenly and stared at her. 'Did you kiss me just now?'

'Yes.' She was in retreat, drawing back from him and wondering what had caused her to behave in such a way. 'I ... I wanted to wake you up.'

'Why? To ask me silly questions?' he challenged her, his eyes glinting between half-closed lashes.

'No ... er ... that is ... I ...' She broke off as he moved and raised his head to look down at her. Lifting his hand from her arm where it had been resting, he stroked her cheek.

'I think I like waking up and finding you in my bed in the morning, all pink-cheeked, dewy-eyed and shy,' he murmured, and then his mouth was on hers, forcing her lips to part. At once passion leapt within her. Her senses spinning, she responded to the caress of his hands with caresses of her own. Slowly, deliciously, her body seemed to be melting into a lovely dangerous softness over which her mind had no control.

A loud banging sound jolted her into stiffness again. Denzil stiffened too, raised his head and glanced towards the door.

'Who's there?' he called out.

'Josh. Wake up, man!' Josh's voice was breathless, urgent. 'Der's a yacht in trouble off de coast. She's

131

driftin' towards de rocks on the southern headland. She's one of ours, looks like de schooner *Mary Jane*. If you want to save her you'd best be coming, boss; Denzil, is you in dere, man? Or is you dead?'

'I'll be with you in a minute,' Denzil yelled. He looked down at Tory, murmured dryly, 'That was quite an experiment you were conducting. Maybe one day we'll be able to complete it.'

He rolled away from her and off the bed. Grabbing his white pants off the chair, he pulled them on over the boxer shorts he had worn to sleep in, zipped them up and buckled the belt. From a drawer he took a shirt and pulled it on. From the floor he scooped up his canvas sailing shoes and went from the room, not even glancing at her as he closed the door.

Alone, Tory rolled on to her stomach and tried to quell the throbbing of her body and the clamouring of her thoughts. What had made her tempt Denzil to make love to her for the second time? Why did her senses take over whenever she was near him? She had never felt like this with Magnus or with any other man. It was a wonderful exciting feeling, but dangerous, especially when it was caused by someone as tough as Denzil whose emotions, she was sure, were iron-bound and were never allowed to get out of control.

Gradually excitement died down and she slept again, only to waken with an alarmed feeling that she had overslept and would be late for work.

Climbing out of bed, she yelped with pain as her right foot touched the floor. She sat back on the edge of the bed and examined the greenish-purple swelling between the ankle-bone and the instep. Somehow she must find something with which to bind it, and she remembered suddenly that Denzil had had a sprained ankle when she had first met him. A search of drawers and cupboards brought to light an elastic bandage and the wooden crutches. With the ankle securely bound by the bandage and the crutches adjusted to her height, she went through to the living room and sat down by the telephone, intending to phone Magnus and tell him that she would not be in to work until later. But the phone was still out of order.

There was nothing else she could do but wait for Denzil to return, and that might not be for hours, depending on how long it took him to bring the yacht in. Feeling hungry, Tory decided to make herself some breakfast. Or was it lunch? she wondered with a rueful glance at her watch. It was almost noon.

She was sitting at the counter on one of the red-topped stools eating an omelette and drinking coffee when she heard footsteps coming up the steps to the back door and the sound of voices, Denzil's and Josh's. She could not move fast enough to be out of the room before they entered, so she tried to appear nonchalant, as if she had every right to be wearing Denzil's beach robe and sitting in his kitchen eating her breakfast, and she pretended she didn't notice Josh's eyes go wide with shocked surprise when he saw her.

Immediately he turned to go back through the door.

'See you later, man,' he muttered, and the screen door clanged after him.

Denzil removed his yachting cap and hung it on a peg near the door, then turned and grinned at her.

'You've shocked Josh,' he said. 'Like most islanders he has very strict ideas about the conventions. Is there some coffee in that pot?'

'Yes. I hope you don't mind, but I made myself some breakfast. Can I make some for you?' she offered shyly.

'Now that's very nice of you, Victoria,' he replied with a touch of mockery, 'but coffee will do. You shouldn't be moving about too much on that ankle.'

He perched on a stool beside her, took a long swig of coffee and set the mug down.

'Is the schooner all right?' she asked.

'Yes, we managed to get a line on her and tow her in. The steering gear is damaged. That was some storm, but it should be the last we'll have for some time.' He flicked her a sideways glance. 'Have you decided what you're going to do?'

'Before I can do anything I must have my clothes,' Tory said firmly.

'Where are they?'

'I left my cases in the hall at the Director's house. They were too heavy to carry a long way.'

'I'll go and fetch them for you,' he said practically, and tilted his mug to drain it. 'You make good coffee, Victoria.'

'But you can't go and fetch my clothes,' she exclaimed.

'Why not?'

'Well, imagine what Rita Jarrold is going to think if *you* turn up and ask for my cases.'

'She'll imagine that you're living with me,' he said with a sardonic slant to his mouth. 'Could be that's not a bad idea.'

'But I can't live with you! I want to go on working at the Gardens,' she protested.

'Doing one—that is, living with me in this house— would enable you to do the other, as I see it.' Denzil's eyes were bright and challenging. 'It could be the answer to your present dilemma.'

'I don't see how.'

'Simple really. Tory, will you marry me?'

Eyes wide, mouth agape, she could only stare at him.

'No, I'm not drunk or crazy,' he murmured with a faint smile tugging at his mouth, obviously remembering, as she was, their first meeting. 'Why the consternation?'

'You're not ... I've never thought of you ... you don't seem to be the kind of man who gets married,' she said confusedly. 'Oh, Denzil, surely you of all people don't feel you have to marry me just because I spent the night with you?'

'I'm not sure I like the implication behind that "you of all people",' he remarked, his eyes narrowing dangerously. 'But you're correct in assuming that I'm not asking you to marry me just to protect your reputation. I want to marry you because I want you to live with me. I told you when we first met I was looking for a woman to share my bed and board, and that you seemed highly suitable. I haven't changed my mind. I like the way you look, I like being with you and I want you in the physical sense. This seems as good a time to ask you as any.'

'But they aren't very good reasons for getting married,' she parried.

'Can you tell me of any better reasons?' he countered.

Tory was silent because she couldn't think of any other reason except love, and after her recent disillusionment concerning her feelings about Magnus she wasn't sure she knew what love was any more. And some inner sensitivity prevented her from mentioning it to Denzil in case he made fun of her.

'Well,' he prompted, 'what's your answer? Will you?'

'I don't know,' she muttered. 'I've never considered getting married to anyone before.'

'Not even to your professor?' he queried, and she shook her head negatively.

'Put him on a pedestal and worshipped at his feet, did you?' he jeered. 'Look, if you're not satisfied with my reason for wanting to marry you you can take an even more practical approach. Marriage to me will provide you with free lodgings close to the Gardens so that you'll be able to continue to work here. It'll give

135

the lie to any suspicions Rita Jarrold might have about your morals and it will make legal something which is going to happen between you and me sooner or later anyway.'

'What's going to happen?' she exclaimed in all innocence.

'Oh, come on, Tory, don't pretend ignorance of the sexual attraction we have for each other. You've been fighting it ever since we met. I've struggled a bit myself, which is why I nearly turned you away last night when you arrived on my doorstep. But I know when I'm licked. I'm ready to give in. So are you, only you're letting those built-in inhibitions of yours get in the way.'

'Oh! How do you know all this?' she exclaimed.

'Give me credit for having more experience than you have,' Denzil growled.

'Oh, I do, I can,' she flared. 'I can give you credit too for being a conceited domineering male who believes that women have been created solely to cook your meals and keep your bed warm!'

'Hell, are we going to have a lecture on Women's Lib now?' he snarled savagely, sliding off the stool and striding away to look out of the window. 'The trouble with brainy women like you is that you don't recognise your own biological urges any more. If it hadn't been for that damned schooner you'd know about them by now. I'd have made sure that you did.'

Tension quivered suddenly between them like a live wire. A hand to her cheek, Tory stared at his broad back and wondered how she could tell him that she knew all about those biological urges when she was with him, but that marriage meant more to her than having those urges satisfied. Marriage meant making promises to love and to cherish. It meant keeping those promises.

Denzil turned slowly to look at her from under frowning eyebrows, hooking his thumbs in the front pockets of his pants.

'I can't offer any more,' he said rather stiffly. 'Take it or leave it.'

'I ... I ... need time to think about it,' she answered rather wildly. 'You see, marriage will give you rights and I ... I'm not sure whether I want you to have those rights over me.'

He swore softly, exasperatedly, lifted his hands in a helpless gesture and let them fall to his sides, then turned away to the door.

'Okay, so marriage would give me rights over you,' he said tautly, 'and I'm not going to pretend I won't use them. But don't forget it'll give you a few too. I'll go and fetch your clothes now. I'll be back in about fifteen minutes. That should give you time to *think*.'

By herself once more, Tory clutched her head with her hands. Marriage to Denzil! A proposal from the last man she had expected to propose to anyone; from a tough freedom-loving adventurer who would surely grow restive under the restraints marriage imposed.

Unless the woman he married could make him feel that accepting those restraints was worthwhile. The woman he married. That would be herself if she accepted his proposal! Should she accept it? Wouldn't she be guilty of marrying him for wrong reasons if she did? To gain free lodgings for herself while she helped Magnus to finish his book. To prevent her contract from being broken!

While she rinsed the dishes she had used, dried them and put them away, Tory went over the reason Denzil had given her for wanting to marry her. He wanted her to live with him. He had wanted that ever since he had met her. Had he seen marriage to her as the only way in which he could achieve that aim?

His proposal baffled her. It just wasn't in keeping with what she knew about him; there must be some other reason. She was still wrestling with her thoughts when he returned with her cases. He carried them into the bedroom for her and went back to the kitchen to make himself some lunch. Quickly she dressed in cool grey linen with touches of white. She brushed her hair and made up her face, then using the crutches she went back to the kitchen. He was sitting at the counter, eating.

'Did you see anyone when you went to the house?' she asked.

'I had the pleasure of meeting Mrs Jarrold,' he replied with a touch of irony. 'She wanted to know if you'll be staying with me permanently. So do I want to know.'

Tory glanced at him warily. He was looking at her with hard clear eyes.

'You know the conditions,' he went on coolly when she didn't answer. 'You can live here for free, but only if we're married.'

'Denzil, I don't understand. I ...'

'You appreciate all I've done to help you,' he interrupted her roughly. 'I know that, but appreciation isn't enough. I want you, on my terms. Yes or no, Victoria?'

'Oh, I can't possibly give you an answer until I've seen Magnus,' she parried desperately. 'He ... he just might have some alternative to offer. Please, would you take me to the Gardens? I can't walk that far on crutches.'

Denzil stared at her and the cold light of hostility was in his eyes. He looked as if he hated her and she had a feeling that he might refuse to drive her to the Gardens.

'Okay,' he said, and she felt herself sag with relief.

'I'll take you to work on one condition.'

'What is it?'

'That you promise to give me an answer at five o'clock.'

'Very well. I promise.'

Magnus was just coming down the wide shallow steps of the white house when Tory stepped out of the jeep. Denzil didn't wait but turned the jeep in a tight circle and drove away down the driveway.

Seeing her on crutches Magnus came across to her, looking very worried.

'Tory, my dear, whatever happened to you?'

'I twisted my ankle. Not much damage, but it's painful to walk on. Magnus, I'm sorry I wasn't able to get to work this morning. I came as soon as I could.'

He studied her face for a second, then glanced in the direction the jeep had gone.

'Mmm, we'll talk in my office at the lab building,' he murmured. 'There's a lot to discuss.'

As they moved slowly in the direction of the lab building he chatted about the tropical storm of the previous night, and of the damage the rain had done to some of the experimental crops. Looking around her as she swung along on the crutches in the serene golden light of the midday sun, Tory thought it was difficult to imagine the dark violence of the storm. Only scattered leaves and petals and glinting pools of muddy water on the path were evidence that wind and rain had streaked devastatingly across the island.

In Magnus's book-lined office she sat down with a sigh of relief. Walking with crutches was tiring and made her arms ache. She watched him take a chair on the other side of the desk and lean forward to fiddle absent-mindedly with an old-fashioned paperweight made in the form of a bird.

'Tory, what happened last night? Why did you leave the house and where did you go?' he asked.

She told him clearly and simply, starting with Rita's visit to her room, and watched him flinch and wince in reaction. When she had finished he sat hunched and frowning, staring at the paperweight.

'It's really most distressing,' he murmured at last, and she wondered whether he meant it was distressing for her or for him. 'I told Rita yesterday that she had nothing to get upset about, that you're a nice young woman with nothing in your behaviour or your way of life to suggest that you go in for permissiveness.' He frowned and worried the paperweight with the tips of his fingers. 'But just now, when I was having lunch with her, she told me that Hallam was here this morning to collect your cases and that you stayed the night with him. That was hardly wise in the circumstances, was it?'

'But I've told you why I went to his house. I'd hurt myself. I was in a mess and there was nowhere else to go,' Tory replied steadily. 'I ... I wasn't very well and I had no clothes ...' She stopped because Magnus's eyebrows went up, in pained amazement, and realising the futility of trying to explain any more, she sighed frustratedly.

'If only you'd gone to someone other than Hallam for help,' he said.

'To do that I would have had to have walked another two miles, you know that, and I couldn't,' she retorted. 'Anyway, I can't see what difference it would have made.'

'Rita would have no grounds on which to base her objection to your continuing to work here,' he muttered.

'I don't see what it has to do with her,' she flared. 'I left your house, which was what she wanted. Where I stayed the night is none of her business.'

'I know, my dear,' he said with a harassed sigh, and ran his fingers through his longish, greying red hair. 'But Rita is making everything you do her business because she's jealous of you. Oh, I know too that she has no cause to be jealous,' he added hastily, 'and I've told her that too. But she has the inflammable latin temperament plus the islander's strict moral sense. You stayed the night alone with a personable single man, a man who has already shown that he doesn't care a snap of his fingers for the opinion of others, and so she's threatening to have you dismissed from your position with the department on the grounds that you're promiscuous.'

'Promiscuous?' exclaimed Tory. 'Oh, really! She must be out of her mind!' She saw his face stiffen and added quickly, 'I'm sorry, Magnus. I know she's your wife, but what she's implying is absolutely ridiculous. She can't have me dismissed on those grounds.'

'I'm afraid she can, Tory. God knows I'd give anything to prevent it from happening because I realise that it's partly my fault you're in this mess. I should never have arranged for you to stay in my house.' Again he ruffled his hair and gave her that rather weak, wry smile. 'I'm afraid I never think how people will react to certain situations, but the contract does say that you can be dismissed from employment by a government department if your work is found to be of poor quality or if your morals or your loyalty are in doubt. Now I can vouch for your work and your loyalty. I can vouch for your morals too, or could have done if Rita hadn't learned that you'd stayed the night at Hallam's house. Unless you can come up with something that will prove that your relationship with Hallam is above reproach, I'm afraid I'm going to lose the services of a very able botanist.'

141

Tory sat in silent dismay. Rita Jarrold held the whip hand. She was an islander, a much-loved and celebrated islander who had an influential father, and Magnus had to step carefully because he himself owed his job as Director to his wife's influence. At least he had admitted to having been responsible for putting her in this difficult position! The other person who was partly responsible, she realised with a little sick feeling of desolation, was Denzil, who had admitted to Rita Jarrold that Tory had stayed the night with him.

Now she knew the meaning of the saying 'to be caught in a cleft stick'. But Rita Jarrold's accusation was so unjust! Anger blazed up in reaction to that injustice. She could not allow her good name to be besmirched in such a way. She couldn't let Rita get away with it, even if it meant committing herself to Denzil's not so tender mercies. Tory raised her head and looked at Magnus with the light of battle in her clear grey eyes.

'I think Mrs Jarrold has insulted me by her implication,' she said coolly. 'She is also going to look very silly when it's pointed out to her that on the night *she* insisted that I leave your house, I stayed the night in the bungalow of the man I'm going to marry.'

Magnus's blue eyes grew round with amazement.

'You and Hallam?' he croaked.

Tory smiled, feeling curiously lighthearted. Now she had the right to tell Rita Jarrold where she could take her suspicions.

'Yes. We're ...' It would be better if she said 'we', she decided. 'We've been considering it for a while. You're the first to be told. Aren't you going to wish me happy?'

'Yes, of course, but ...' Magnus looked thoroughly confused, almost shocked. 'Tory, marriage is a very serious business and ... what I'm trying to say is ... I hope Hallam hasn't taken advantage of ...' He broke off, red-faced and embarrassed.

Yes, he has, she thought to herself, but not in the way you're thinking. Aloud she said,

'You will tell Mrs Jarrold as soon as possible, won't you? I wouldn't like her to make a fool of herself through ignorance of the true state of affairs. Denzil has a very hot temper, and if he hears what she's been implying about me he might be very unpleasant to her.'

'Yes, of course he would, quite rightly so too,' Magnus muttered, and mopped his forehead, which was suddenly beaded with sweat, with his handkerchief. He rose to his feet and went to one of the windows to pull down the venetian blind as a protection against the warm rays of the afternoon sun which had begun to slant into the room. 'Tory, it would be as well in view of what's happened if you and Hallam could marry soon. It would make it easier for me ... for you, for everyone concerned.' He turned round, looking more worried than ever. 'You'll continue to work even when you're married? I mean, he isn't going to be awkward and say you can't work here, is he?' he demanded anxiously.

'I think I'll be able to persuade him to let me continue to work for you,' she replied, keeping her head down to hide her amusement at the change in his attitude. 'But will the department be prepared to employ a married woman?'

'Oh, yes. No problem there,' he said, and came back to his chair, sounding almost hearty now that he had seen how his problem could be solved. 'Whew, it's very warm in here, but I'd like to get down to work. Your news about your forthcoming marriage, though startling at first, has taken a load off my mind and I can now apply myself to the book. It's really suffered this week, what with Rita's return and all the upset that's caused.'

Tory watched him and listened to him, and soon she was absorbed in the work of classifying and describing the Caribbean members of the largest and most important group of garden plants in the world, namely the pea family of herbs, shrubs, trees and vines. There were over seventy-three genera of the family to be found in the islands and most of them were loved for their spectacular blossoms, such as the flaming red and yellow poincianas and the delicate vivid bauhinias or orchid trees, of which there were a hundred and fifty species.

Time passed quickly, and at quarter to five Magnus called a halt. Tory brought her mind back from the world of carpels and stamens and faced up to the reality of meeting Denzil in fifteen minutes and telling him that she would marry him, the sooner the better.

He arrived in the jeep just as she was leaving the building. He turned off the engine and waited for her to approach. When she had reached the vehicle she stopped and rested on the crutches. From under his cap brim he slanted her a speculative glance.

'Well? Did your dear professor come up with an alternative proposition?' he asked, the scorn he felt for Magnus showing as always in the curl of his lip.

Tory stared at him and wondered if it were at all possible to get beneath his tough hide, jolt him into showing his real feelings.

'Denzil, what would you do if I told you I don't want to marry you?' she countered with a question, and watched him carefully for his reaction, but apart from a fractional narrowing of his eyes he showed nothing.

'I'd turn on the ignition, engage first gear and drive away without you, and you'd have to find your own way to Port Anne,' he replied coolly. 'Is that what you're going to tell me?'

'No, it isn't. Oh, don't you ever show how you feel?' she demanded crossly.

'Sometimes,' he admitted laconically, 'but not here, not now. I gather the answer is yes.'

'Yes!' Tory hissed the word at him through clenched teeth and he grinned aggravatingly at her.

'So once again the professor failed to come up to scratch,' he scoffed. 'Too bad, Victoria. Get in and I'll take you to a hotel, and book a room for you until we can sign that contract.'

'What contract?' she asked as she settled herself in the seat beside him.

'The marriage contract, lover, the one which gives me rights. Remember?'

'I remember,' she answered tautly, 'but there's just one thing I want you to know before I sign it.'

'And that is?'

'I'm marrying you because I want to stay on Airouna and finish the work I came to do, because I don't want my contract to work broken, and for no other reason. Is that clear?'

'Perfectly clear, Victoria,' he replied, his hands on the ignition key. 'It's what I thought you'd say.'

CHAPTER SEVEN

A WEEK later Tory opened the screen door of Denzil's bungalow and entered the living room. It was half-past five and she had just returned from the botanical gardens where she had worked with Magnus all afternoon.

It had been an afternoon like any other afternoon on the island. It had sparkled blue and yellow, warm but not too hot because of the steady trade wind that blew. But there had been one difference: although she had started the day as Victoria Latham she had spent the afternoon as Victoria Hallam.

She glanced into the living room. It was as usual shady, its combination of sea and citrus colours giving an impression of coolness. No one was there. She peeped into the kitchen; it was empty. Josh, who had come in the jeep to pick her up from the lab building, had told her that Denzil had gone out to sea to test the engines of a new motor cruiser and would be back soon.

Quickly she went to the bedroom. Her cases were there. She would unpack, hang her clothing in the closet, take a shower and dress in something cool and flowing, her new caftan, perhaps. By then he should be back.

It had really been easier to get married than Tory had thought. Denzil had agreed that they should do it as soon as possible and had set about acquiring a licence. Even so, she had been surprised when he had arrived at the lab that morning and said that they were to attend at the registrar's office within the hour. She had gone with him and had found the brief civil ceremony simple and undemanding. Afterwards he had taken her back to work, telling her he would settle her account at the hotel where she had stayed for the past few days and would take her cases to the bungalow. On her return to work Tory had told Magnus that the fact had been accomplished, shown him her wedding ring, had received his rather diffident congratulations, and plunged almost immediately into the classification of the next most common Caribbean family of plants known as the four o'clock, which included the old-fashioned verbena and the splashy-coloured purple, crimson, orange and white bougainvillaea vines.

Fait accompli. The phrase rolled round Tory's mind as she shook out her clothes and hung them in the long built-in closet next to the few suits of Denzil's that hung there. She was married, her contract was safe and only at the risk of creating a scandal could Rita Jarrold do anything about it. What now?

She would have to write and tell her parents. She could see no way of avoiding that because she would have to tell them of her change of address. And then there was the possibility that they might take a winter holiday and fly out to the island to see her. In fact, once they knew of her marriage they would probably insist on coming out in order to meet Denzil.

What would they think when they learned she had married a man she had mentioned only once in her letters to them, briefly, in that last letter she had written the night Rita Jarrold had made her leave the Director's house? Tory could almost hear the words her mother would use to describe her action—headstrong, stubborn, wilful. And what would they think of Denzil?

She imagined her father would like him and accept him without question just because he sailed boats, but her mother would want to know all about him; where he'd been born, which school he had attended, whether his parents were alive, whether he had any brothers or sisters, why he had left England, did he intend to return? Oh, the questions would go on and on, and Denzil would be rude.

What was the use of thinking about it? Tory pushed the niggling thoughts to the back of her mind. She was married, and why she had married and whom she had married were no business of anyone else.

Grabbing a towel and her toilet bag and flinging her caftan-like housecoat over her arm, she left the room to go to the bathroom. In the passageway she paused, hearing voices coming from the living room. Quietly she walked towards the room and peeped round the corner to see who was with Denzil. She couldn't see anyone because they were either in the kitchen or in the dining recess, but she could hear the clink of ice against glass and the bubbly sound of liquor being poured into a glass.

'Yes, sir,' boomed a deep voice which she recognised only too well as belonging to Peter de Freitas. 'It really took the wind out of our sails when Mandy and I came up here to look for you this morning and Josh told us you were in town getting hitched. Who's the lucky bride? Not that blonde girl you brought to Tequila a couple of weeks ago?'

Tory couldn't hear Denzil's answer and she assumed he had turned away from the counter, possibly to return the ice tray to the fridge. Knowing she was doing the unforgivable—eavesdropping—she stepped a little further into the living room to hear better.

'Well, Mandy's going to be pleased when she knows,' Pete growled. 'She likes that kid. But I never thought I'd see the day when you'd throw in the towel and get married. I always had the impression you weren't entirely hooked on the idea of being tied to one woman.

And knowing what a tricky guy you are, I wouldn't be surprised if you'd married her to suit some deep and devious plan. Cheers.'

'Cheers,' said Denzil coolly. There was a small silence while they drank, then he said slowly, 'Actually I married her because she was in one hell of a spot and needed help.'

'Ha?' Pete's laugh boomed through the house. 'No, Denzil, that's doing it too brown. You're not the chivalrous type. I refuse to believe you married that lovely girl to help her out of a spot. Don't forget I saw the way you kissed her on your boat at Tequila.'

'Well, I admit that my motives in marrying her are not entirely quixotic,' replied Denzil mockingly. 'I expect to be rewarded for the service I've rendered.'

'You expect to be re ...' The rest of the word was lost in a guffaw of laughter, and with cheeks suddenly flaming Tory turned on her heel, ran into the bathroom and closed the door with a slam which shook the wall and was probably noticed in the dining recess.

Hands to her ears, which were burning, she watched the water run into the bath. No wonder they were burning, she thought. She had eavesdropped on a conversation between two men who were friends and had heard something she would have preferred not to have heard.

But what would she have preferred to have heard? Would she have liked Denzil to be less honest and tell Pete that he had married her because he was in love with her? Oh no, that would be too silly, because she knew he wasn't in love with her. But she would like him to be.

The thought came crashing crazily into her mind as she stepped into the bath, pulled the shower curtain across and pressed the button which diverted the water from the taps to the shower outlet.

Why was she thinking that way? She had gone into this marriage with her eyes wide open, knowing why Denzil wanted to marry her, so why was she wishing now it had been for another reason—for love?

Love, love, love, all you need is love, the song which Tory had heard so often sung by the Beatles jangled round her mind as the water sluiced down over her head and body and she searched for a reason why she wished Denzil had married her for love. She found it as she turned off the shower. If he told her he loved her, it would be so much easier for her to reward him in the way he expected.

The doorknob rattled as someone turned it and tried to push the door open, but failed because she had locked it.

'Tory? Are you in there?' Denzil asked.

'Yes. I'll be out in a minute.'

'No rush. Pete's here and has invited us out to dinner with him and Mandy as a sort of celebration. Is that okay with you?'

'Yes, yes, of course. I'd like that.'

In the bedroom she took her time to rub her hair dry and change into the blue evening dress. When she went into the living room the two men, having consumed several drinks, were in a frivolous mood and after he had persuaded her to have a drink, Denzil went off to shower and change, leaving her to deal with Pete's teasing and sometimes risqué remarks.

They went by taxi to the home of Mandy's sister in the Portuguese quarter of the town where Mandy and Peter were staying the night, and were invited into the pleasant old wooden house with its high sloping tiled roof and tiny wrought-iron balconies.

There more drinks were offered and consumed and it was decided that Mandy's sister and her husband should also come out to dinner, and soon they were all jammed into a taxi and on their way to the fisherman's wharf. Tory found herself sitting on Denzil's lap because there was no room for them to sit side by side, and the touch of his hands, one at her waist and the other on her bare arm, made her suddenly aware of the change in their relationship which had come about that day. She sat stiffly, her face averted from him, her heart beating wildly as she wondered why she had allowed herself to be trapped into marriage with him.

In the restaurant they ate delicious seafood and drank champagne, and danced to the beat of bongo drums. Tory ate, drank, danced and laughed with the rest of them, trying to ignore the remark of Denzil's which she had overheard earlier: *I expect to be rewarded for the service I've rendered.* Was he really so cold and calculating?

She turned to look at him and found he was in conversation with a thin young woman who had a cloud of fluffy brown hair. He was smiling rather mockingly at the girl, who seemed to be pleading with him, and when he suddenly realised that Tory was watching him he leaned forward and said loudly, to make himself heard above the noise of the drums and guitars:

'Tory, this is Moira Townsend. She works in the British Trade Commissioner's office. Moira, I'd like you to meet Tory, my wife.'

The young woman, who was, Tory judged, about two or three years older than herself, turned quickly, eyed Tory assessingly then turned back to Denzil.

'It's true, then?' she said.

'Some of it is true,' he replied, and rose to his feet. 'I'll be back in a minute.'

He walked off in the direction of the washrooms and Tory was left alone with Moira. Mandy, Peter and the other couple were all dancing energetically.

Moira turned back to Tory. She had big brown eyes,

a turned-up nose and a wide mouth that looked as if it did a lot of smiling.

'I'm pleased to meet you, Tory,' she said. 'Denzil and I ... well, I used to think we were good friends.' Her thin shoulders shrugged. 'I couldn't believe it when I heard today that he was married. You see, he's always made it very clear to any woman he's dated here that he's just not the marrying kind. Of course, once I heard all the story I realised he had no option but to help you out of a hole.'

'What story have you heard?' said Tory, finding that her lips were suddenly dry.

'That the Director's wife turned you out on the night of the storm last week and you had to spend the night at Denzil's place. A bit like jumping out of the frying pan into the fire, if you ask me,' said Moira with a giggle.

'Where did you hear the story?'

'Oh, in a roundabout way really. The sister of one of the girls in the office goes about with Dr Jarrold's daughter. It seems she was full of the story and was telling everyone. Something of a narrow squeak for you! You could have found yourself out of a job. The government departments are very sticky here about the behaviour of their female employees. Lucky you to have Denzil come to your aid. How long do you think you'll be able to make it last?'

'Make what last?'

'Why, your marriage to him, love, your marriage!' Moira's eyes were as sharp as a bird's as she tipped her head sideways so that she could see Tory's face better, and Tory felt an instinctive urge to run and hide from that enquiring gaze. 'I mean, it isn't off to a very good start, is it? Anyway, let me know when you're thinking of packing it in. I wouldn't mind having the opportunity of comforting Denzil when you've gone.'

She went off with a wave of her hand, and feeling a little sick Tory leant an elbow on the table and her head on her hand. Everyone knew why Denzil had married her. Their marriage was probably the subject of gossip in every government office, and all because of Carla's far-reaching malice. She couldn't bear the thought of everyone gossiping and sniggering. She couldn't bear the thought, either, of going back to the bungalow with Denzil, knowing that he had the right to make love to her; knowing that he would now expect her to submit to him as his reward for having helped her.

Gathering up her evening bag, Tory stood and walked out of the noisy room. She went through the small foyer and out on to the wharf. In the water of the harbour, reflected lights shivered as the wash made by a fishing boat, leaving to go to sea for the night, made ripples fan out on the surface, and the ropes holding other boats against the stone wall squeaked as their captives bobbed up and down as if eager to leave too.

Tory walked blindly, not really sure of direction until she found herself on a narrow lane that curved beside a silvery moonlit beach overhung with coconut palms. Turning off the lane, she slipped off her high-heeled sandals, and carrying them in her hand plunged her feet into the warm silky sand. Right to the edge of the water she walked, where it fell in sighing little waves against the shore. She paused for a moment, then stepped into the water. It slopped over her feet, bringing them a tingling ease and wetting the hem of her gown.

'Tory.' Denzil's voice spoke just behind her, imperatively. 'What the hell are you doing?'

His hand on her bare arm was rough, and he jerked her round to face him. He was a square dark shape against the glimmering moonlit sand that stretched behind him.

'Why did you leave the restaurant?' he demanded.

'I felt a little sick—the champagne, I think, and it was too hot in there,' she explained woodenly. His fingers gripped hard. She raised a hand and pushed back the hair from her face. 'I didn't know anyone had seen me leave,' she whispered.

'You mean you hoped *I* didn't see you leave,' he corrected grimly. 'You were running out on me, weren't you, on our wedding night?'

'Oh, there wasn't a wedding in the proper sense. Our marriage isn't real,' she cried out.

'It's real to me,' he growled roughly, 'and I'm taking you back to the bungalow now to show you just how real it is.'

'No, Denzil, I can't. I won't!' she twisted desperately, trying to break his hold on her arm. He grabbed her other arm and jerked her forward so that her head fell back, then his mouth came down on hers in a bruising, forceful kiss.

'Yes, you will,' he murmured against her lips. 'And stop fighting me, Tory. You'll only get hurt if you don't.'

Turning, Denzil pulled her along behind him over the soft sand. She resisted as best she could all the way to the lane, but she was no match for his strength. At the edge of the sand he kept hold of her while she slipped on her sandals, then he took a tighter hold of her arm so that she was forced to walk beside him. Suddenly limp and without energy, Tory felt like a puppet being supported like a puppeteer.

At the wharf, as always, there were a few taxi-cabs lingering hopefully to look for tourists coming out of the restaurant. A whistle from Denzil brought one to his side. He opened the rear door, pushed Tory inside and gave instructions to the driver. In the smoky darkness of the cab he didn't touch her, nor did he say anything. The silence seemed to throb with their unexpressed hostility. What a way to begin a marriage! *Not off to a very good start, is it?* Moira Townsend's words seemed to mock Tory.

Lights glared at the marina and as they walked up the path to the bungalow she heard music blaring from someone's radio. An outboard motor started up, and its put-put sound was thrown back in echoes from the other side of the bay.

Up the steps, through the door Denzil marched her, never letting go of her arm once. In the living room she tried to pull away, but his grip didn't slacken. Down the passage to the bedroom they went. He pushed open the bedroom door, flicked on the light and propelled her into the room and let go of her at last. He took the key out of the lock.

'Get undressed and into bed,' he ordered crisply. 'I'll be back.'

The door closed after him and she heard the key turn in the lock. Hands to her face, her breast rising and falling with the tumult of outrage, Tory stared at the door. Ever since she had collided with Denzil on the ferry boat she had been trying to avoid this moment. At that first meeting she had thrown up defensive blocks to protect herself against their attraction to each other. Since then every meeting with him had turned into a confrontation as she had struggled to prevent his complete domination of her mind and body. Now she was at the last ditch and she could see no way out.

Slowly she began to undress. She had just taken out her nightdress, long and peach-coloured, made from sheer chiffon nylon, when the key turned in the lock and the door opened. Clutching the nightgown against her bareness, she backed away. Denzil closed the door and turned; his jacket was over his arm and his white shirt was undone, the purity of its colour and the crispness of the material contrasting starkly with the dark tan of his torso.

'I said undress, not dress,' he murmured, his glance on the nightdress, and he turned away to hang his jacket in the closet. Quickly Tory flung the nightgown over her head and thrust her arms through the armholes, and scooped up her toilet bag from the dressing table.

'I'd like to clean my teeth,' she said.

He was pulling off his shirt. Muscles rippled under the tanned, hairy skin, and as she watched she felt a twinge of desire in the region of the pit of her stomach.

'Okay,' he said, 'you do that. I'll be waiting in the passage for you to come out of the bathroom, so no thinking up any more getaway tricks.'

He stood at the doorway of the bedroom and watched her go along to the bathroom. Tory took as long as she could over washing her face and hands and cleaning her teeth. She did think of trying to escape through the window, but common sense suddenly asserted itself. Where could she go if she escaped? Nowhere.

Denzil was leaning against the wall waiting apparently patiently when she opened the door and stepped out into the passage, and he followed her back to the bedroom on bare silent feet. He kicked the door closed after him and as she turned from dropping her toilet bag on the dressing table she found him there right behind her, a big-shouldered man whose skin gleamed in the oblique light from the bedside lamps, and whose eyes twinkled and danced with mockery as he stared at her.

'Ready now?' he asked softly.

'Denzil, I can't,' she said rather weakly. The closeness of him was having its usual effect on her, making her legs shake and her arms want to reach out to hold on to him.

'Yes, you can, lover,' he murmured, putting his arms round her. 'I'm going to show you how.'

They stood face to face like enemies. He stepped closer and Tory felt the hard thrust of his body against hers, smelt the musky smell of male hair and skin as he bent his head towards her, felt a sensuous tingle spread through her as his lips touched the delicate curve where her neck and shoulder met. Involuntarily her body arched against the thrust of his and as he felt that response, he gathered her up in his arms and carried her to the bed.

There she tried to roll away from him, but a long arm reached out and the chiffon of the nightdress tore apart with a soft hiss under the pull of his ungentle hand. Once again face to face but now lying down, they stared at each other challengingly, then the dark glitter of his eyes was hidden as he glanced at her mouth. As his lips possessed hers again he lifted her hand in his and placed it palm down against his chest. Liking the warm pulsing feel of him, she slid her hand down of its own volition, smoothing it against the cool curve of his waist and the sinewy hardness of his thigh.

Desire was swelling slowly within her, threatening to take over. She made one last effort to resist it.

'I don't want to be a reward,' she complained, snatching her hand away from him.

'What the hell are you talking about now?' he exclaimed.

'I heard what you said to Peter,' she muttered.

'So that's why you slammed the bathroom door,' he accused. 'See what happens when you eavesdrop? You get half a story and usually the wrong half. Pete was being nosy about us, too personal, I was trying to put him off. I made him laugh and so was able to change the subject without him feeling as if I'd snubbed him. We didn't discuss you any more.' He blew gently at the tendrils of hair which clustered about her brow. 'Was that why you were going to walk into the sea?' he teased. 'Just because you didn't like the idea of being a reward?'

'It wasn't only that. Carla has been telling everyone that you had to marry me. Moira told me. They're all gossiping about us.' Her voice shook a little.

'And that troubles you?'

'Yes, because it isn't true, is it?'

With the point of his forefinger he traced the line from the tip of her chin, under it and down her throat so that delicious shivers shook her. His hand slid down further, pushing aside the torn chiffon to curve under her breast. Her senses swam and she pressed closer to him, luxuriating in the slightly sticky feel of her skin as it rubbed against his.

'No, it isn't true,' he said. 'I married you because I want you to live with me, and don't you forget it, and the way we're going to do it, it's going to be as much a reward for you as it will be for me.'

Sensuous pleasure swelled within her, searching for a way out. She flung her arm around him and smoothed the powerful curves of his back with her hand.

'Oh, Denzil, I do love you,' she cried, and knew she meant it with all her heart.

'Now you're getting the idea,' he scoffed softly. His mouth came against hers again as he pushed her back against the mattress so that he could lean over her, and slowly, tenderly the passionate persuasion of his lips and hands brought her feelings to bursting point for which there seemed no release. But release came as he took her, in a lovely flowing feeling compounded of pain and ecstasy, and as they lay in each other's arms in a state of drowsy relaxation Tory understood what

Denzil had meant about their union being as much a reward for her as it was for him.

Being together next morning was both a joy and a torment; a joy because they both remembered the pleasure of the previous night, a torment because they woke late and had to hurry, with the result that they argued about who should use the bathroom first, who should make breakfast, and about how Tory would get to work.

'I can't take you and bring you back every day,' Denzil snarled as the jeep hurtled round bends, and Tory felt she was in danger of being thrown out into the hedge of myrtle and wild poinsettia which edged the road.

'You don't have to,' she replied with dignity. 'I'll buy a bicycle and ride it.'

That silenced him and not another word was spoken. In front of the big house he let her off, then drove away in a cloud of pale dust. For a moment she stared after the vehicle feeling a flicker of insecurity, wondering whether now he had got what he wanted from her he would treat her carelessly, taking for granted that love that she had expressed so impulsively in the night.

Her confession of love for him had disconcerted her. She had not realised she loved him: so many times she had thought she had hated him for his arrogant intrusion into her life. Yet he had admitted nothing of love for her. He had admitted only that he had married her because he wanted her to live with him, share bed and board, something that Tory was sure other women would have done without marriage.

She turned away to walk to the lab building. The door of the house opened and a husky voice called to her.

'Miss Latham ... oh, I beg your pardon ... Mrs Hallam, I'd like a word with you, please.'

Rita Jarrold stood on the top step, a slim figure in a dark red caftan-style housecoat, leaning against one of the white pillars which supported the portico.

Tory waited at the bottom of the steps.

'I'm a little late for work, Mrs Jarrold,' she replied politely. 'Couldn't we talk later?'

'What I have to say won't take long,' said Rita as she pushed away from the pillar and came down the steps. She moved with a feline sinuousness and her gold slippers glinted as she walked. When she reached the bottom step she stopped so that her eyes were on a level with Tory's.

'I suppose you think you've been saved from losing your job by marrying that ruffianly adventurer who manages the marina,' she drawled.

'Denzil maybe an adventurer, but he isn't ruffianly,' retorted Tory, conveniently forgetting that she had once considered Denzil to be a ruffian. 'He's a well-bred man who cares about other people.'

'And you believe he cares for you, no doubt,' said Rita mockingly. 'I can scarcely credit that a young woman of your intelligence and upbringing has allowed herself to be blackmailed into marriage with a man about whom nothing is known. Why, you've no idea where he's been or with whom he's been.' Rita shuddered slightly with distaste, as if Denzil were a stray cat or dog.

'If that's all you have to say I'll be on my way,' Tory said in a stifled voice as she tried to control the anger boiling up inside her. 'I've no wish to listen to you insult my husband.'

'I wasn't insulting your husband. I was just stating facts, and I want to warn you that you still have to step carefully. I shall be keeping a close watch on you and your dealings with my husband, so don't think for one moment your marriage to Denzil Hallam has altered my opinion of you.'

Tory turned away and ran, not wanting to hear any more. She was convinced now that Rita was not just physically ill but also mentally disturbed. Surely no one in their right mind could carry spite to such lengths? Having failed in her attempt to remove her from her job, Rita was now trying to rouse her distrust of Denzil.

Her breathless arrival in the lab brought kindly jeers from the other botanists who congratulated her on her marriage. Soon she was absorbed in her work, writing a talk to be given to a women's church group in a village in the north of the island. Rita Jarrold's remarks were forgotten, and for a while so was Denzil, but towards five o'clock Tory began to feel anxious, recalling his testiness of the morning. He might not come for her. He might forget to send Josh for her if he couldn't come himself. Although her ankle was much better she didn't fancy trying it out on the pathway over the hill. She supposed she could call a taxi, but she would have to pay for it to come out and pick her up as well as for conveying her to the marina.

All her anxiety vanished as she left the lab building and saw the blue jeep waiting. She kissed its smiling driver with joyous abandon and settled into the seat beside him.

'I've bought a present for you,' Denzil said as they charged round the bends of the road.

'Oh, I forgot! I didn't buy one for you,' she exclaimed, surprised that he had even thought of a wedding present.

'That's okay. I didn't expect one.'

'What is it?' she demanded.

'Wait and see,' he taunted. 'There's no fun in giving presents or receiving them unless they're a surprise.'

Never had the sky seemed so blue, the trees so green, the water in the bay so glitteringly inviting. This was what being in love felt like; this soaring of the spirits, this contentment to be where she was as long as he was there too. And he had bought her a present.

When Tory saw it leaning against the steps of the bungalow her delight knew no bounds. It was a motorised bicycle, the sort used by many of the islanders and hired by tourists as an economical way of getting about.

'I don't know how to thank you,' she exclaimed, turning to him.

'Never has one moped aroused so much joy,' he scoffed. 'You can give me my reward later ... tonight.'

Not every day began so unpleasantly and ended as happily. Squabbles between them blew up quickly like tropical storms, but they often ended in shared laughter or lovemaking. As the days became weeks Tory became aware of changes in herself. She was not so inclined to retort angrily to Denzil's remarks, but considered them first to find out whether they were made in fun or whether they were serious, for he often teased her unmercifully. When she found that he was very particular about everything being kept in its right place she tried to be more tidy, and noticed on his part less of a tendency to snarl at her every time she left her books or clothing scattered about the place. They were adjusting to each other in many ways, and as time went on her happiness seemed to create a golden capsule around her, making her immune to contact with other people. People like Magnus and Rita and Carla were still there, still played a part in her life, but they no longer had power to hurt her.

With the end of November and the approach of Christmas the tempo of life on the island quickened slightly as more tourists arrived. Business increased at the marina so that sometimes Denzil went away for a week to skipper one of the yachts himself. The first time it happened Tory spent a miserable first night longing for him with an intensity which alarmed her. It wasn't right to become so dependent on him, she warned herself, because he was probably enjoying himself in some yachting haven and not longing for her.

Christmas came and she decorated the living room of the bungalow with huge crimson pin-wheels of poinsettia which she had gathered from the Gardens. It was odd to spend the day sailing in bright sunshine over dancing white-crested water, to swim in a secluded cove and sunbathe on a shimmering crescent of white sand, to eat barbecued steak from cattle raised on the island instead of turkey, and fragrant golden mangoes instead of plum pudding.

Cards had arrived from relatives and friends. Even Denzil had two, one from his grandmother and another one from Cornwall which had been signed simply 'Wanda', followed by the message 'See you soon'.

Looking through the cards after they had returned to the bungalow on Christmas night, Tory teased Denzil about the message.

'Who is she?' she asked. 'Someone from your never-to-be-related past?'

'Yes.' The answer was curt, pushing her away.

'Do you think the message means she's coming to visit you soon?' she persisted, ignoring the danger signs.

'I don't know.'

'Would you like her to visit you?'

'Tory, why don't you shut up about it?' He got up from the settee where he had been sitting and moved rather restlessly about the room.

'I'm sorry,' she faltered, 'I'd no idea I'd touched such a tender spot.' Then she added in a low voice, 'You must have loved her very much.'

For answer he swore viciously, opened the screen door and went out. Tory heard him pound down the steps and then there were only the sounds of the night and the rustle of leaves, the croak of frogs and the distant shushing of waves.

Tory placed the card back on the side table where she had set out all the cards, and bit her lip to hold back the tears which rushed to her eyes. Why had she made the last remark? She knew very well why. She had been hoping he would turn to her and say something like—'I did love her once, but it's all over now. I love you.'

She was always hoping that he would say he loved her. But now she could only think he was still in love with a woman called Wanda, who was coming to see him, Why, then, had he married *her*?

She sat for a while waiting for him to return, but the day of sailing had its usual effect, making her sleepy, and she went to bed. She fell into a doze almost at once and didn't hear Denzil come into the room, but was disturbed by his quiet movements as he undressed in the dark.

She raised herself up on her elbows and peered through the dimness.

'Denzil, are you all right?' she whispered.

'What do you mean by all right?' he growled.

'I've been worried about you. You went off without a word and were a long time coming back. What have you been doing?'

'Drinking.' The mattress sagged beneath his weight as he lay down beside her.

'Oh, why?' Tory was more worried than ever now. 'It was my fault, wasn't it? I shouldn't have said what I did . . .' She broke off because she could feel him shaking with laughter. 'What's so funny?' she demanded.

'You are,' he replied, putting an arm out and drawing her down to him. She smelt rum on his breath and the tang of tobacco smoke. 'You're so easy to tease,' he murmured. 'I went for a walk and called in on Josh, had a drink with him and his wife, that's all; and you get all worked up thinking I'd been drinking to forget something unpleasant.' His mouth touched hers and as always his passionate persuasion roused an answer within her and the strange little disturbance was forgotten.

But she did not forget the message in the Christmas card entirely, and every day when the ferry or the small charter planes brought a new load of visitors to the island she half expected to find a woman called Wanda at the bungalow when she returned from work. January passed without anyone coming. February brought crowds of visitors to see the usual Mardi Gras festival and a letter came from her mother saying that her parents couldn't see their way to afford a trip to the island in March as they had hoped.

Tory was surprised at her own disappointment. She hadn't realised she had been looking forward so much to their visit. As a result she suffered from a bout of homesickness, and longed passionately for the soft gentle rain of northern fells. One evening she babbled to Denzil about snowdrops and primroses, and about the carpets of daffodils beside the lake where her parents had their summer cottage.

'Perhaps you should take a holiday and go over,' he murmured. He was writing to his grandmother again. 'Surely your contract provides for some time off?'

'I don't know, I'll have to look at it. If I took a holiday and flew home, would you come with me?' she asked.

'Not this time of the year. It's too busy here. It would be best if you went on your own, saw all your friends and killed that nostalgia for good and all. It's the only way.'

'What if I didn't come back?' Tory challenged, a

little hurt by his refusal to accompany her.

'You'd break your contract, wouldn't you, lover?' Denzil retorted lightly, and turned back to his letter.

Looking at the contract she found that it did provide for her to have two weeks' holiday in the year, and so she asked Magnus if he would mind if she went to England. He was disconcerted, as usual, at the thought that something might interfere with his work, but agreed reluctantly and Tory went ahead to make the arrangements to fly from Antigua in two weeks' time.

She didn't really want to leave Denzil, because she found she felt a little insecure where he was concerned. There was just the possibility that he might leave Airouna while she was away, sail off into the blue and not come back. She had noted a restlessness about him lately, a withdrawn mood which brought all her doubts about him to the surface of her mind to nag at her.

She was packing her clothes late on the day before her departure for Antigua by ferry when she heard footsteps come up the steps to the front door, followed by a gentle tapping on the frame of the screen door.

She went to open the door and at the sight of a woman standing with her back to the door, dressed in a smart striped cotton dress, she hesitated. The woman turned and looked through the mesh screen.

'Oh, hello,' she said in a very English voice, 'I'm looking for Denzil Hallam.'

'He's away just now, at sea,' replied Tory. 'Won't you come in?'

She swung back the door and the woman, who seemed to be about ten years older than herself, stepped by her.

'I'm Tory Hallam.'

The woman, who was small and dainty, swung round and her deep blue eyes widened.

'Hallam? You did say Hallam?' she queried.

'Yes. Denzil and I have been married for nearly five months.'

A prettily-shaped mischievous-looking mouth curved into a smile.

'I'm Wanda Trelawney, and I was divorced from Mark Trelawney ... let me see now.' She put one finger of her white-gloved hand to her smooth pink cheek as she thought. 'Yes, it must have been about five months ago. How strange,' she added, smiling again. 'I wrote and told Denzil and said I'd be coming to the Caribbean. I have relatives in Grenada.'

'I see.' Wanda seemed very pleasant and was amazingly colourful with her dark blue eyes and red-gold hair. 'Please sit down,' added Tory. 'Would you like some iced tea?'

'Thank you.' Wanda sat down on the edge of an armchair and looked about the room while Tory went into the kitchen to make the drink. When she returned to the living room with the drink she said chattily,

'As a matter of fact I'm just packing to go to England to visit my parents for two weeks.'

'I wouldn't if I were you. The weather has been awful, quite cold and wintry, down in Cornwall anyway,' replied Wanda. 'You sound as if you come from the north.'

'Yes, I do.'

'Then how did you get out here?'

Quickly Tory gave a résumé of how she had come to Airouna.

'I must say you're a bit of a shock to me,' said Wanda when she had finished. 'I'd no idea Denzil was married. I don't think his family do either. I saw his brother only the other day in Falmouth, and told him I was coming out here and hoped to visit Denzil. I'm sure he would have told me if he'd known about you. Has Denzil let his grandmother know?'

'I ... I don't know.'

'Oh, if he has you'd have heard from her by now. She's like that—always very particular about doing the right thing like sending birthday cards and so on. She would have written to you personally. I wonder why he's kept marriage to you a secret?'

The dark blue eyes had lost their good-humour and were surveying Tory critically. 'Denzil has never talked to you about me, has he?' was Wanda's next very pertinent question.

'No.' How foolish she was beginning to feel at having to reveal that she knew nothing about her own husband.

'I thought not.' Wanda watched her own slim red-tipped fingers as they smoothed the tassel on a cushion. A faint enigmatic smile quivered about her mouth. 'I'm the reason he left England,' she announced rather smugly.

'I'm afraid I don't understand.'

The dark blue eyes lifted to look at her rather pityingly.

'We were in love,' said Wanda with a wistful sigh, 'but I was married to Mark. I'd married him when I was eighteen. He was much older than I, more than twenty years, and I thought him quite fascinating at the time. But as the years went on the difference between our ages began to tell.' The pretty mouth curved in another gamine smile, 'I like to enjoy myself, to dance and flirt. I used to go to the local yacht club quite often, with friends. I met Denzil there.'

'Did he know you were married?'

The dark blue eyes glanced away. Wanda sighed wistfully again.

'I wore a wedding ring, dear, so he must have known, mustn't he?' she replied rather dryly. 'Anyway, my husband found out about our little affair. It caused quite a scandal in our part of the world.' Wanda laughed as if she had enjoyed being the central person in a scandal. 'It also caused trouble in Denzil's family. I believe he had a row with his uncle. Anyway, the next thing I knew he had left in his yacht to sail across the Atlantic. His family, the Hallams, are very wealthy, you know.'

'No, I don't. In fact I don't know anything about them,' said Tory stiffly, watching her guest ease on her gloves.

'Well, there aren't many of them now. Denzil's parents were killed in an accident when he was young. His grandmother brought him up. There's his Uncle Trevor and his brother Garth, who is much older than he is … about fourteen years, I should think, and then of course Granny Hallam who's an absolute dear. When do you expect Denzil to come back?'

'Later this evening. Perhaps you could come and see him tomorrow. I'll tell him you're here.'

'That's awfully nice of you—considering,' said Wanda, rising to her feet.

'Considering what?' The woman was really quite tantalising.

'Considering I'm no longer married to Mark. What a pity Denzil didn't receive my letter before he married you … not that I've anything against you personally, you seem a nice enough girl … but he's in love with me, and we always used to say that if ever I found some grounds on which I could divorce Mark, we'd get married.'

Wanda left and Tory returned to her packing. The sun set in its usual blaze of glory. She ate her dinner alone, then Josh came to tell her that he had talked to Denzil over the ship-to-shore radio, and that Denzil had said he could not get back until the next morning; and she went to bed feeling miserable because he hadn't bothered to return for her last night on Airouna.

In bed she lay awake thinking of Wanda. She had explained so much about Denzil, particularly his concern for herself when he had realised she hadn't known about Rita Jarrold. *Think you're the only one who has been in this situation?*, he had jibed once only to find himself trapped in the situation with her, marrying her to enable her to keep her job, only to learn, too late, that the woman he loved was at last free.

Tory tossed and turned all night, wishing he was there to answer her questions and stifle her doubts with his kisses, but he wasn't there, and he didn't arrive until she was ready to go to the harbour to catch the ferry.

He came straight to the bungalow from the big schooner which he had been skippering and came through the door just as she was about to go through it.

'I'm sorry, lover——' he began, but cross because she had slept badly and was anxious, Tory snapped at him,

'I bet you are! It shows how little you really care. You didn't even try to be here.'

'Look, Tory,' Denzil took hold of her shoulders, but she wrenched herself free.

'I'll miss the ferry and the connection at Antigua if I don't go now,' she cried, 'and then you'll be stuck with me like ... like a gooseberry when your real lover comes to see you.'

'What the hell do you mean?'

'Wanda ... the ex-Mrs Trelawney is here in Airouna. She came because she thought that now she's free you and she could get married, the way you had it planned back in the old days when she was still Mrs Trelawney.'

'Shut up!' Denzil's voice was savage and his eyes blazed with green fire. 'You don't know what you're talking about.'

'That's not surprising, is it, since you've never told

me anything about yourself? So you were caught stealing another man's wife ...'

'That isn't true!' he thundered. 'Tory, for God's sake will you shut up and let me explain?'

'It's too late. There isn't time.' She clattered down the steps. Josh was waiting in the jeep in which her cases were already stowed. Denzil came after her, leaping into the back of the jeep as it shot forward. The ride to the ferry was a silent one apart from Josh, who like all islanders sang or hummed when he was working or driving.

The ferry was just about to cast off the warps which held it to the wharf when they arrived. Josh jumped out of the jeep and ran ahead to ask the captain to wait.

'Tory, you can't go like this,' Denzil's voice was low and held a note of desperation.

'Yes, I can, and I am. You can have your sweet Wanda to yourself!'

'You're coming back.' It wasn't a question, it was an arrogant statement of fact as he moved to stand in front of her and blocked her way. She looked up into hard clear eyes that glared down at her furiously and once again it seemed to her he was standing in her way like an immovable rock.

'Oh, I don't know. I can't think. Please let me pass,' she muttered wildly.

Denzil moved and she dodged round him to follow Josh, who was carrying her cases to the gangway where they were taken by one of the crewmen. As she hurried up the gangway, Tory heard Denzil call after her, his voice clear and cutting.

'Tory, if you don't come back I'll never forgive you!'

She was aware of heads turning, of eyes staring at him, then at her, then she was on the boat and the embarkation gate was closed and the engines were throbbing in reverse. Quickly she moved along to the bow of the boat so that she could see the wharf. Perhaps if she waved, made some signal such as kissing her hand to him, he would know that she intended to come back. But among the small group of people standing there waving farewell to the ferry she could recognise only one, the tall gentle black man called Josh. Denzil had gone.

CHAPTER EIGHT

Towards the end of her first week in England Tory caught 'flu and suffered the usual aches and pains, shivers and sniffles. Since she was enjoying herself visiting all her friends and relatives, she gave herself only a couple of days to get over the illness. Then, through 'sheer neglect', as her mother put it very forcibly, she went down with a severe infection of the lungs that developed into pneumonia. By the time she was able to sit up and take nourishment again she was lighter in weight and she had been away from Airouna for over three weeks.

'I've written to Dr Jarrold and to Denzil to tell them why you haven't gone back,' said her mother. 'They should have received the letters by now. I wrote on the Monday you should have flown out and posted them the same day, so you should be hearing from them soon.'

But all Tory could think was that Denzil would believe she had run out on him.

Slowly she began to pick up strength, and soon she was able to take walks in the garden, well wrapped up against the cold March winds which blew in off the Atlantic across the flat fields of south-west Lancashire. Every day she looked for a letter from Denzil, and once or twice she tried to write to him to tell him that she was making progress. But each time she started to write she remembered the threat he had flung at her across the space between the ferryboat and the wharf at Port Anne: then she would think of Wanda, and wonder whether it was better not to write, to let him think she had run out on him, let him sue for divorce and be free to marry Wanda.

So she never finished her letters, but screwed them up into tight balls and dropped them in the waste-basket.

She had been in England four weeks and was still under the doctor's care when two letters came from Airouna. One was from the Department of Parks and Gardens cancelling her contract with them because she had overstayed her leave. It was signed by the head of the department; Harold Ribiera, Rita Jarrold's father. The other letter was from Magnus.

His untidy scrawl brought him into the room, attractive, diffident, wryly smiling, hoping she would understand that he hadn't been able to do anything about re-negotiating her contract. He had hoped that she would return to Airouna anyway, to be with her husband. However, he had heard recently that Hallam had left the marina and it was now under new management. He assumed that Hallam had gone to England to join Tory there, so he could hardly expect her to come back to the island and help him finish the book. It was a pity, because she understood the way his mind worked and ...'

The letter dropped from Tory's suddenly nerveless fingers. Denzil had left Airouna. When? Why? Where had he gone? Frantically she picked up the letter from the floor to read it again, hoping that there would be some indication of when he had left and where he had gone. As she straightened up a wave of nausea hit her, turning her dizzy, then everything went black and she fell.

She came round to find herself lying on the chaise-longue in the sitting room, and to see Dr Jones entering the room followed by her mother.

'Well, young woman! What have you been doing now?' he asked.

'I must have fainted,' she muttered. 'I remember feeling sick.'

'Let's have a look at you,' he said. 'No, not the lungs this time.'

Tory glanced across at her mother, who was standing by the window. Pamela smiled at her reassuringly.

'I'm sure everything is all right, love, but it's just as well to have a check-up.'

The doctor was gentle, as he was always, and when he had finished the examination he sat on the edge of the chaise and took one of her hands in his.

'Do you know you're pregnant, Tory?' he asked quietly.

Again she glanced in the direction of the window, but her mother had gone, was in fact just closing the door of the room behind her.

'I thought I might be,' she murmured.

'About two and a half months, I'd say. Are you pleased?'

'Yes.' It came out rather forlornly. 'Don't tell my mother, please, I'd like to tell her myself.'

'Of course you would. It's your business, after all,' he said as he got to his feet. 'I'd like you to come down to the surgery next week for a proper ante-natal check up before you go back to the Caribbean. No chance of you staying in this country to have the child, I suppose?'

'There might be,' she said.

When he had gone she lay and stared at the twigs of forsythia tapping against the window. The tiny yellow flowers were just beginning to show. By the time Denzil's child was born it would be autumn. Panic streaked through her, causing her to sit up quickly. She was going to have Denzil's child and she had no idea where he was!

Perhaps a letter would come from him soon, telling

her of his whereabouts. Unless he had gone to sea again, or—pain twisted knife-like through her—unless he was with Wanda. Oh, if only Magnus had been more explicit, less vague—but then Magnus cared only about plants, about his wretched book. Sobs shook her suddenly. *Oh, Denzil, Denzil!*

'I've brought you a cup of tea, love.' Her mother's matter-of-fact voice broke through the storm of emotion. 'Now whatever is the matter with you?'

Tory gulped, wiped her eyes and took the tea-cup and saucer.

'The government of Airouna has cancelled my contract because I overstayed my leave.'

'Oh, how silly of them! Surely your Dr Jarrold can put it right? Once you're back there I'm sure something can be done.'

'I'm not going back.'

'But, Tory, you must. You're married to Denzil.'

'He isn't there. He's left, and I don't know where he is. It's in Magnus's letter. Oh, Mummy, what am I going to do?'

'Well, just now you're going to drink that tea,' her mother said. 'Then you're going to wash your face and comb your hair and have some lunch—Robin and I have had ours. Then you're going to help me pack for tomorrow. Remember we're catching the early train for Penrith so that we can reach the cottage in the afternoon. We're going to be busy for the next few days to get everything warmed up and ready by the time your father and George come up on the Thursday.'

'But supposing a letter comes from Denzil while we're away?'

'Your father will bring it with him when he comes. Now buck up, love, I'm sure there's a good explanation for what's happened. Maybe Denzil is on his way here. You know the post has been most peculiar lately. I'm

176

sure we haven't received all the letters sent to us.'

Tory tried to feel reassured by her mother's calm attitude, and even managed to enjoy the journey north the next day; a journey she had made every Easter and every summer holiday for as long as she could remember.

The brown fells lifted to a pale blue sky, looking as remote and as mysterious as they had always done, and the lakes glinted with wan silvery light. The small stone cottage looked solid and squat and as always, its windows brimmed with gold when the sun set. All night the nearby beck rushed noisily over the rocks and eventually its tinkling sound lulled Tory to sleep in the room she shared with her sister.

The next few days passed in peace as fires were lit, beds were aired, furniture was polished and dishes and glassware were washed. In the garden crocuses, yellow and purple, thrust through the winter-bleached grass. In the woods primroses and wild violets peeped from hiding places under silver birches drooping pale catkins. The sun grew warmer as the week advanced, and March gave way to April, and by Thursday the daffodils were bursting yellow from their pale beige sheaths.

On Thursday afternoon Tory was sent to pick daffodils from the edge of the lake. She squatted to pick them because bending made her feel sick. Every morning she examined her waistline to see if there was any change; so far she had not told her mother.

'Tory, Tory, Dad's here!' Her sister Robin was running down the hill from the cottage, her blonde hair flying out behind her. 'He's brought someone with him besides George, and Mum says you're to come *at once*. She said it just like that. No argument. You're to go *at once*.'

'Who's he brought?' asked Tory, leaning forward to take the steep slope.

'Oh, I dunno, some man. I didn't get a chance to find out 'cos Mum sent me to get you. Come on, hurry up! George has brought his girl-friend. You'll never guess what her name is. It's Priscilla, and that's worse than Victoria!'

With that parting taunt she rushed off. Tory followed slowly. Once she had been able to run up the hill like Robin; now it made her breathless just to walk up it.

She went in through the kitchen and left the daffodils in the sink. Hearing Pamela talking in the sitting room she went though to it and stood stock-still in the doorway, her eyes wide and incredulous; because the man who was there listening politely to her mother, and who was wearing a dark brown suit of corded velvet, had dark curly hair which grew down his lean cheeks in long sideburns.

'Denzil,' she said, and he turned to give her a hard unsmiling stare.

'I'll leave you two alone for a while,' said Pamela diplomatically. 'We'll be having tea soon.' She went out, closing the door firmly behind her.

'Denzil, what are you doing here?' exclaimed Tory foolishly.

'I'm not quite sure,' he replied coolly. 'Your father seemed to think it was a good idea for me to come.' He glanced round the cosy, over-furnished room and flexed his shoulders as if he felt trapped in it.

Tory was trying to control an urge to fling herself against him, to hug and kiss him, but he looked and sounded so very unforgiving that she didn't think that such a move on her part would be welcomed by him at that moment.

'Where did you meet him?' she asked.

'At 36, Lilac Avenue, where he lives,' he replied

dryly. Where do you think? Tory, why are you so thin?'

'I've been ill—I had pneumonia. That's why I didn't return to Airouna when I should have. Mum sent a letter to you, explaining. Didn't you get it?'

'No. It must have arrived after I left and it hasn't caught up with me yet.'

'When did you leave?' she demanded.

'A few days before you were due to arrive. I sailed in *Ariel* to Antigua to meet you. I thought we'd have a good time sailing back, but you didn't get off the plane, so I decided you'd run out on me and I didn't bother to go back to Airouna. I went on to St Thomas and handed in my resignation as manager of the Airouna marina. While I was there I received a message from my brother. He'd phoned me at Airouna and Josh had told him where I'd gone. My grandmother was very ill and asking for me. So I left *Ariel* in St Thomas and flew to London. I arrived in Cornwall in time to see Gran die; I was there until last Tuesday, then I had to go to Manchester on business for my brother. It seemed a good idea to call on you and find out what had happened to you.'

His terse, coldly-spoken sentences gave her no hope. He hadn't come to England to see her, and wouldn't have come if his grandmother hadn't died. That was very clear. And he wouldn't be here in the cottage if his brother hadn't wanted him to go to Manchester on business.

'I ... I'm sorry about your grandmother,' she said weakly, and sat down on the old love seat that her mother had bought for a few pounds at a local auction sale and had re-upholstered in red plush herself.

He didn't sit down beside her but stood with one arm resting on the mantelshelf of the old stone fireplace, looking down at the flames which flickered there. The crackle of the fire and the occasional flop of ash in the hearth were the only sounds in the room.

'Denzil, I didn't run out on you,' Tory said suddenly.

'But the thought crossed your mind,' he shot back at her.

'Only because of what Wanda said.'

'Which you didn't give me a chance to refute.'

Oh, he was hard all the way through, she thought, like the rock of Gibraltar to which she had compared him at their first meeting. How on earth could she get him to understand how she had felt the day she had left Airouna?

'She said you were in love with her and not with me. She said that if you'd received her letter telling you she was divorced and free to marry you, you wouldn't have married me,' she said steadily, keeping her gaze steady on Denzil, expecting him to turn and tell her that what she had said was true.

'I did receive her letter before I married you,' he replied quietly, and continued to watch the flames.

'Oh!' It was all very puzzling. 'Then why did you marry me?'

He turned at last to look at her, but the expression in his eyes hadn't changed; they were still as hard and clear as an eagle's.

'I seem to have spent the last few months answering that question,' he said with a touch of exasperation. 'I married you because I wanted you to live with me.'

'But not because you loved me.'

'It amounts to the same thing.'

'No, it doesn't. Loving means sharing, helping, cherishing, accepting the other person's failings ...'

'And what the hell do you think I've been doing ever since I set eyes on you but helping you, protecting you, accepting your silly female wilfulness, sharing all I had with you? Good God, Tory, what else do I have to do to prove to you that I love you?'

He spoke harshly, but her heart bounded in her breast and was no longer a dead weight, and it seemed that the colours of the room grew brighter and warmer.

'All you ever had to do was tell me,' she said simply.

'Well, I'm telling you now,' he growled. 'How was I to know you'd believe a frivolous shallow woman like Wanda more than you'd believe me?' he added bitterly. 'You even believed her story that I tried to steal her from her husband.'

'Didn't you?'

'No, she just made it appear that way to clear herself with him. Oh, I admit I was fascinated by her for a while, in the same way you were fascinated by Magnus Jarrold. She's a few years older than I am, but when I first met her that only made her more fascinating. She was pretty, charming, experienced and fun to be with. I thought she was a widow and was sorry for her because she had been widowed so young. I was shocked when Trelawney appeared that night at her house and said he was her husband. You see, she'd told me he was her father-in-law.'

'Oh, how naughty of her!' Tory found she could not help being amused by the trick the mischievous Wanda had played. 'But how awful for you, I expect your feelings were very hurt,' she added, thinking how she had felt when she had found out about Rita Jarrold.

'It was my self-esteem that took the worst blow,' he said, and the slightest of smiles tugged at one corner of his mouth. 'Especially when I discovered I hadn't been the only young man she had entertained in her "father-in-law's" house. But I soon got over it.'

'She told me she was the reason you left England!' exclaimed Tory.

'Did she?' Denzil laughed rather scornfully. 'She

must have sized you up pretty well then. She guessed you'd fall for a romantic angle like that. No, my leaving at that time was just coincidence; I'd been planning to sail across the Atlantic for some time. Just after I'd found out about Wanda I had a row with my uncle about the business management of the pottery.' His mouth curved sardonically. 'As usual he won, and I decided I was wasting my time trying to fight his old-fashioned notions of business, so I left on the next high tide.'

'Pottery?' she queried. 'Whose pottery?'

'Hallam's Pottery.' He glanced round at the wooden plate rack which ran round three walls of the room and on which Pamela Latham displayed pieces of antique pottery and china and glass, which she had either inherited or had picked up at sales. His roving glance came to rest on a dinner plate on which there was a design in blue. He crossed the room, reached up and lifted it down and studied it.

'I was right,' he said complacently. 'It's one of my great-grandfather's most popular designs, called Blue-bell Mist.'

'Oh, let me look, please.'

He came over and sat beside her handing her the plate. She admired the delicately-painted design of bluebells round the edge of the plate and handed it back to him.

'Mum is going to be very thrilled when she learns you're related to *that* Hallam,' she said.

'Makes me respectable, does it?' he scoffed, placing the plate on a side table. 'One of the reasons why I left home the way I did was that I was tired of being made up to by people like Wanda because I'm a Hallam. You see, in my part of the country the name carries weight, and is always associated with money.'

'But I don't understand why you stayed and managed the marina in Airouna,' she complained.

'I'm the youngest of the family. I could have stayed at the pottery as a hanger-on, with a position but no real work, no power, never getting a chance to prove that I could do more. My uncle Trevor managed the business side. My brother Garth was, and still is, in charge of design. There was no opportunity for me to do anything until my uncle retired. So I had to find something else to do. Sailing across the ocean alone helped to satisfy some of the urge, but when I'd done it I had to find something else. Developing the marina, building up the chartering business offered a challenge ... for a while. I was thinking of packing it in and going on another long-distance voyage when you turned up.'

'I wish you'd told me all this before,' she said. 'You could have told me on Christmas night when I asked you about Wanda. Why didn't you?'

He leaned forward, his arms resting on his knees, his hands clasped loosely together as he stared at the fire.

'I suppose I didn't because I was unsure of you,' he said gruffly.

'Why?' Tory was amazed at his confession.

'We were married in rather peculiar circumstances and I could never be sure whether you'd married me because you liked me or whether it was because you wanted to keep your job. I didn't tell you about Wanda in case you were disgusted by my youthful foolishness. I wasn't sure you'd understand about her. And I was right, you didn't understand, and you wouldn't even let me explain why I hadn't been able to get back the night before you left for England.'

His voice was hard again, unforgiving.

'I was upset,' Tory said in a low voice. 'You see, I was unsure of you too. You'd been so restless and I thought you were regretting having married me ...'

'It wasn't that. It was the marina. The place was running smoothly and had lost its challenge,' Denzil explained quickly. 'God, Tory, if you knew how I felt when you didn't get off the plane at Antigua you wouldn't doubt my love for you. I was convinced you weren't coming back to me.'

Was it her imagination, or had his voice cracked a little under the pressure of his feelings? The longing to touch and hold him was too much for her. Reaching forward, she ran her fingers under the thick hair clustering at the nape of his neck. Slowly Denzil turned his head to look at her, and leaning towards him she kissed him on the mouth. As soon as they touched passion exploded between them, and they leaned against the back of the love seat, their hands caressing each other gently as if each were afraid the other might disappear.

'Tory, Mum says to tell you tea's ready,' Robin's high voice came clearly through the panels of the door and Tory broke the kiss to answer.

'We're coming!' she called back, and turned to Denzil again. 'I was coming back to you,' she whispered, 'but I couldn't help being ill. I ... I'm going to have a baby.'

The clear hazel eyes, so close to her own, blinked once, twice, then widened slowly.

'Mine?' he whispered incredulously.

'Of course,' she snapped. 'Surely you don't think ...'

'Hell, no! I didn't mean it that way. I'm just a little shaken. I've never imagined myself as a father.'

'You don't mind, do you?' she asked, suddenly anxious. It had never occurred to her that he might resent having a child.

'No, I don't mind because it will be ours. But what about you? Do you mind? You're the one who has to have the child, not me.'

'I'll be all right as long as you're there. You will be there, won't you, when it's born? You won't go away?'

'I'll be there. No one is going to stop me from seeing our son born.'

'Daughter,' she argued promptly.

'Why is it you love to disagree with me?' Denzil taunted, his mouth hovering threateningly above hers.

'Tory, Mum says the meal will spoil if you don't come *at once*,' Robin called again. 'Come on, you two. I can guess what you're doing. Break it up, break it up!'

'We'd better go,' muttered Tory, sitting up and smoothing her hair back.

'Not yet,' he said autocratically, pulling her back beside him. 'First things first. Where are you and I going to sleep tonight?'

'Here, I suppose.'

'Your mother was saying something to me about being cramped for space and that she'd have to put me in the same room as your brother because there are only three bedrooms, and the girl he brought will have to sleep in yours. It's just not good enough, Tory. I'm sleeping with you.'

'Oh, you can't. Robin and I share a bed and Priscilla will be on the folding bed.'

'Then we're leaving. We'll find a room in the hotel I noticed at the head of the lake. Is it any good?'

'First class, but it's very expensive and select.'

'So what? At least we'll get some privacy. And that brings me to the second matter we have to settle. Would you mind if the child is born in Cornwall?'

'Is that where we're going to live?' she asked.

'That's what I hoped you'd say, lover,' he retorted with a grin. 'That's where I'm going to live, and I hope you'll be living there with me. My uncle has decided to retire at last, and since I've inherited most of my grandmother's loot, which included a substantial number of shares in the pottery, Garth has asked me to take over the management of the business side. Being an artistic type he has no head for that sort of thing.'

'And you've agreed because you never could resist a challenge,' Tory teased.

'No more than you could ever resist playing with fire,' he retorted, standing up and pulling her to her feet so that he could take her in his arms and press her long length against him. 'Can we leave as soon as tea is over?' he whispered in her ear. Then she felt his lips against her throat and their passionate touch sent shivers down her spine, causing desire which had lain dormant all these weeks to uncoil itself.

'I don't think so. They're going to be very hurt as it is when we tell them we're not staying the night,' she replied, leaning against him and rubbing her cheek against his.

'I can't help that,' Denzil retorted roughly, tipping his head back to look at her. 'I have to have you to myself soon, without interruptions. Five weeks without you is too long.'

'Too long for me to be without you, too. Oh, Denzil, I've been so worried not hearing from you, thinking that you hadn't forgiven me for not coming back and maybe if your grandmother hadn't been ill, if you hadn't had to come to England, you wouldn't have come at all, wouldn't be here now,' she whispered, voicing the fear which was uppermost.

Strong fingers curved round her head, forcing it back so that he could look into her eyes.

'I was angry, I'll not deny it, but not with you; with myself for having allowed any woman to mean so much to me. My initial reaction was to go off on another voyage telling myself that you weren't worth so much anguish. But I'd been telling myself that ever since you collided with me on that ferryboat. Every time I made some approach to you and you brushed me off I'd tell myself that the next time we met would be different and I wouldn't let you in to take over all my thoughts and feelings. But we'd meet and I'd find myself relenting, finding some excuse for you, forgiving you. This time isn't any different from the others. When I'd simmered down I'd have come looking for you because you've got to me where it hurts, lover, and I can't do without you.'

Again his voice shook a little with the intensity of his feelings, and overwhelmed by his confession, Tory wound her arms about him and pulled his head down close so she could whisper,

'And that's how I feel about you too, lover.'

He began to kiss her on the mouth, on the cheek, on the eyes on the throat, a rain of short, sharp, shocking kisses which soon had her flushed and breathless and reeling with desire.

'Denzil, please, not here!' she was gasping laughingly, when the door opened and Pamela said sharply,

'Now, look here, you two, you're keeping us all ... oh, I see you're busy.' Her voice softened with amusement.

Denzil raised his head and looked at her.

'Has this daughter of yours told you you're going to be a grandmother?' he demanded.

'Tory! Really?' Pamela was now smiling rather foolishly.

Tory nodded as she tried to smooth her dishevelled hair and cool her hot face with her cooler hands.

'Then I must go and tell Jack at once,' said Pamela, and went from the room leaving the door open.

Denzil, triumphant because his ruse to get rid of her mother had worked, pulled Tory back into his arms, but she held him off, her hands against his chest.

'Please don't think I'm brushing you off,' she teased gently, 'but haven't you realised that the sooner we have tea the sooner we can leave and go to the hotel?'

She watched the twinkle of devilry begin to dance in his eyes as he smiled at her.

'Now you're getting the idea, my darling,' he retorted softly, and hand in hand they left the room to go and join the rest of the family at the tea table.

Harlequin Presents...

By popular demand...
24 original novels from this series—by 7 of the world's greatest romance authors.

These back issues have been out of print for some time. So don't miss out; order your copies now!

Harlequin Reader Service
ORDER FORM

In every issue...

Here's what you'll find:

♥ a complete, full-length romantic novel...illustrated in color.

♥ exotic travel feature...an adventurous visit to a romantic faraway corner of the world.

♥ delightful recipes from around the world...to bring delectable new ideas to your table.

♥ reader's page...your chance to exchange news and views with other Harlequin readers.

♥ other features on a wide variety of interesting subjects.

Start enjoying your own copies of Harlequin magazine immediately by completing the subscription reservation form.

Not sold in stores!